Life as a Cowboy
Life's Outtakes-Year 9

52 Humorous and Inspirational Short Stories

By
Daris Howard

A collection of stories, humorous anecdotes, thoughts, and tidbits of wisdom from the popular newspaper column.

Publishing Inspiration

Life as a Cowboy

Life's Outtakes-Year 9

52 Humorous and Inspirational Short Stories

By

Daris W. Howard

A collection of stories, humorous anecdotes, thoughts, and

tidbits of wisdom from the newspaper column

Life's Outtakes.

ISBN-10: 1-62986-013-1
ISBN-13: 978-1-62986-013-8

www.publishinginspiration.com

Publishing Date:

Publishing Inspiration LLC

Table of Contents

Dear Reader,

People often ask me if my stories are true. Though I must admit that I tend to take a bit of literary license in my writing, each story is based on an actual event. Sometimes the stranger stories are the ones that are stretched the least. As people often say, truth is stranger than fiction.

I also want to note that some of the names have been changed to protect the anonymity of the individuals.

Daris Howard

Life as a Cowboy

When my son was a teenager, he, like many young people his age, was in desperate need of a job. I insisted that my children earn half of the money they wanted for extra things, and I provided work picking and selling raspberries so they could. However, as they grew older, picking raspberries was the last thing they wanted to do even though it provided a decent wage.

My son applied around to different places and soon had a job working at a business that specialized in dairy products. They sold milk, cheese, and the best ice cream in town. My son enjoyed learning to make up cheese sandwiches, cook soup, and create beautiful ice cream cones. There were other tasks that weren't quite as enjoyable but weren't too bad. These included cleaning around the store and stocking the coolers.

But on days when business was slow, he was assigned to a job that he detested. He had to dress up in a cow costume and stand on a busy street corner holding a sign advertising the business. This was almost always done in the summer when the ice cream created an irresistible draw, but it wasn't the hot, sweaty costume that he hated. What he hated was the fact that his friends might find out he was dressed as a cow.

For my part, I was pleased that he was responsible enough to work at something he detested. It showed a willingness to do what he needed to do. There were many times that I did miserable jobs, especially as I was trying to make my way through college, and I did them willingly in order to take care of my family.

When we drove by that intersection where my son stood, my four-year-old daughter was always proud to see her brother there in the cow costume, and she waved enthusiastically at him. He didn't complain about that since most children waved at him, but he drew the line at her calling hello out the window, especially if she used his name. He had thus far been able to conceal his identity, and he wanted to keep it that way.

But one day I took the whole family to eat at a pizza establishment. My four-year-old daughter ran into some friends of hers there, and one of them proudly pointed out that her own sister was a waitress at the restaurant. This soon escalated into a my-family-is-better-than-your-family situation as one girl said her sister worked at another popular restaurant and one said her brother worked at a ranch store.

I was concerned that my little daughter might say something about her brother's job, and sure enough, before I could stop her, she jumped into the conversation with her friends.

"Well, my brother is a . . ."

As she spoke, our whole family braced for her to reveal my son's secret identity, because to her, his secret identity was akin to that of a superhero.

". . . my brother is a *cowboy*," she said.

The rest of our family stifled our laughter until the other little girls had gone back to their families.

When my little daughter joined us back at our table, I asked, "Are you proud that your brother is a cowboy?"

She nodded enthusiastically. Then she looked at me quizzically.

"Daddy, weren't you a cowboy when you were young?"

I smiled. I thought of my days riding horses, branding cattle, and many other such activities, but I could see by the look on her face that an image of me dressed in a cow suit was flowing through her mind.

"Yes," I said. "I was a cowboy."

"Did you get to wear a fun costume, too?" she asked.

"I suppose you could say that," I replied.

"Well," she said, "when I grow up, I'm going to be a cowboy, too."

Army Intelligence

It was the time of the Korean War, and Carl knew that if he didn't sign up for the military, he would be drafted. If he signed up, he would have two advantages. First, he would have a say in what branch of the military he went in to, and second, he could become an officer. He chose the army.

Of course, he had to go through basic training. There he began to wonder about the phrase "army intelligence." It seemed to him like those two words were contradictory, given the feeling that it was him they were trying to kill. But finally, basic was over, and he was stationed in Maryland near where a lot of the army brass lived.

A friend of Carl's told him of an opening leading the army band. Carl was a talented musician. In high school he played in almost every kind of band there was: dance bands, blues bands, and jazz bands. But even beyond his musical talent, he was a born showman. The job was perfect for him, and after auditions, those in charge agreed.

His band mostly performed as the background music at parties for the army brass. The band would play quietly while people visited, ate dinner, or whatever. But one day his commanding officer came to him.

"Lieutenant Atwater, I am assigning you to play at a party for which I am responsible. Many army generals and their wives will be there, along with senators, congressmen, and others. Basically, anyone who is anyone having anything to do with the army will come, and everything has to be perfect. Your band has to play to perfection."

"Yes, Sir," Carl said. "I understand."

"Not only that," the commanding officer said, "it will be a long party, and I don't want you repeating music. You must have a full repertoire. Do a good job, and there could possibly be an advancement coming your way."

Carl was excited. "Yes, Sir!"

The night of the party went along as usual. There were a few long, boring speeches, the regular dinner, and, of course, a bit too much alcohol. The party was really dragging when Carl's commanding officer's voice came over the intercom.

"Lieutenant Atwater, please meet me at the oak tree."

Carl obeyed. His commanding officer was pacing there when he arrived. "Lieutenant," he said, "play some livelier music. The party is dying."

Carl went back to his band, and they started playing what lively music they had. Briefly the party picked up, but because the band mostly played quiet dinner parties, they had soon played most of the upbeat songs they knew. Since he had orders not to repeat anything, they were forced to go back to slower music. Once more, the party began to drag.

Again his commander's voice came over the intercom. "Lieutenant Atwater, please meet me at the oak tree."

Again he obeyed. When his commanding officer asked about the music, Carl explained that they had played all of the upbeat songs in their repertoire except for one.

"Then play it," his commander said.

"But Sir, it's . . ."

His commander didn't even let him finish. "I don't care if it's the North Korean national anthem. Play it before everyone falls asleep."

Carl, who was a bit of a prankster anyway, went back and did as he was told. His band played something that would hit the army officers even more than the North Korean national anthem, and it was far more recognizable. They played "Anchors Away," the Navy theme song. He had to admit that all of the army officers did suddenly come to life. He had barely finished when the speaker boomed out just as he had expected.

"Lieutenant Atwater, meet me at the oak tree."

He never did get the advancement.

A Little Boy Who Needed Softball

My son was born with some health challenges and needed physical activity to help him walk better. So when he was in kindergarten and asked to play softball, I immediately took him to the community center so I could pay the ten dollar fee and sign him up.

The lady there remembered me from my time coaching little girls' basketball and asked me if I wanted to coach my son's softball team. I told her I really didn't have time. But a few days later she called and said they couldn't get anyone else, and if I didn't coach it, they would have to cancel the team. I knew how much my son wanted and needed to play, so I decided I needed to make the time.

I set up a practice schedule, and at our first practice I noticed a small boy sitting across the field watching us. He was there at the next practice, too. When I went to visit with him, he scampered away. At the third practice I could see him there again. I asked the children on the team if anyone knew him.

A boy named David raised his hand. "His name is Timmy."

"Can you tell me about him?" I asked.

David shook his head. "He is home schooled and doesn't play with other kids."

"Would you see if he would like to play?" I asked.

David said he would. He walked toward Timmy, and when Timmy started to run away, David called after him. Timmy stopped, and after they had visited a moment, both boys came walking over.

I had my team start warming up, and I sat down to visit with Timmy.

"Would you like to be on our team?" I asked.

I could see by the look in his eyes that he did. But he just shrugged. "Can't. My dad said we can't afford the fee."

"You're in luck," I said. "Today the fee is taken care of."

He grinned with excitement. "Really?"

"Really," I replied. "Practice with us today, and we'll see about getting your parents to sign the form when we're done." He nodded, so I continued. "Do you have a mitt?" He shook his head. I smiled. "Well, you're in luck there, too, because we have an extra one."

I had rounded up all the extra mitts I could find at the second-hand store. I handed him the last one. It was a bit large, but it worked.

I noticed that Timmy struggled to run and often fell down. I watched him and watched my own son. Their physical challenges were almost identical. Although Timmy wasn't very good, he had a big heart and quickly got up each time he fell.

The others weren't sure about him at first, but I encouraged them, and they were soon cheering him along. When we finished practice, my son and I walked with Timmy to his home to visit with his parents.

When I mentioned I would like to have Timmy join my team, his dad shook his head. "Timmy can't do stuff like that."

I explained about my son's challenges and how the doctor felt physical activity was good for him. "I think it might help Timmy, too," I said. "And I would take good care of him."

Timmy's dad shook his head. "I ain't paying for something that he'll give up on and fail at."

"Oh, there's no fee," I replied. "You just have to fill out the permission form."

Timmy's dad looked at me suspiciously. He glanced at Timmy, who had such a hopeful expression on his face. Then Timmy's mother nodded her desire to let Timmy try, and finally Timmy's dad gave in and signed the paper. I left and immediately took the paper to the community center. Though registration was supposed to be closed, the lady accepted it after I explained the situation.

I paid the fee, and the lady smiled and nodded when I said, "And in case anybody asks, there was no fee."

I knew this was a little boy that needed softball even more than my son did.

Getting Up Each Time We Fall

Coordination was hard for one of my sons because he was born with some physical challenges, and I felt activity would be good for him. I began to coach a softball team so he could play, and when another small boy, Timmy, who had similar problems, started hanging around at our practices, I talked Timmy's reluctant father into letting him play.

I watched as my son and Timmy tried, but stumbled and fell time and time again. And when they tried to bat, the ball was long past before they swung.

I started taking my son to the ball diamond an hour or two before the others showed up so I could help him. Timmy would immediately come over when he saw us. I worked patiently with the two boys. Sometimes I think I felt worse watching them fall down than they did. There were times I wanted to run to them and pick them up, but I knew I couldn't. I always told them, as I told my whole team, "Getting up each time we fall is what makes us stronger."

The two boys did grow stronger and could eventually run all the way to a single base without falling down. For batting, I started having them just hold their bats out, and I would pitch at it. Gradually they started swinging the bat, and eventually they were able to hit the ball. The other children were far better, but each day I could see improvement in the two boys.

When we played our first game, I made sure every child played. It was not important to me if we won. I had only agreed to coach to build children. Sometimes the other children would become frustrated with my son and with Timmy, but I always ran interference. Sometimes parents could be even meaner, but I talked with them before our first game and made it clear how I felt. For the most part they were understanding.

Timmy and my son didn't do too well in their first games, but we continued to work, and they continued to improve. As the season went on, I hoped that Timmy's parents would come. I looked for them at each game, but they weren't there. Timmy's father said he didn't want to be embarrassed. But finally, one day, I heard someone cheering for Timmy and turned to see his mother. She was surprised to see her son chasing after the ball in the outfield, even though he fell down a few times. His throws were a bit wild, but he threw.

Each coach pitched to their own team. I knew right where to put it for Timmy. When he hit the ball and ran all the way to first base without even stumbling, his mother almost fell off the bleachers.

At the last game I was surprised but pleased to see Timmy's father sitting beside his wife. His shock at seeing Timmy run and catch a fly ball was evident. He was soon cheering for his son and was louder than any other parent there.

The years passed, and my wife and I continued to encourage our son. He grew strong, and a person would hardly know he had ever had any problems. But I always wondered what happened to Timmy. Then one day, I happened to be at the high school to pick up one of my daughters when the district baseball championship game was about to start. The team passed me, heading out to the field, when a tall blond boy stopped and looked back. He turned and came trotting back to me. He smiled.

"Hey, Coach. It's good to see you."

I didn't have any idea who he was or why he called me "Coach," so I just said, "It's good to see you, too."

The young man's coach called. "Hey, Tim, you're the starting pitcher today. You better get warmed up."

Suddenly, I realized who the young man was, and my shock must have shown in my expression.

Tim laughed. "Remember, getting up each time we fall is what makes us stronger."

Most of my college students are bright, fun to teach, and hard working. But each semester I get interesting letters, emails, and phone calls from a few students. I save these, and occasionally I compile them into a column. The last couple of years I have shared some of these, and with school just starting, I thought I'd share a few more. I don't think any of these comments need any explanation, other than to say that I changed or removed any names for anonymity. Also, I pared down a few of them a bit.

You know those online quizzes you talked about last week? I thought it was just an attendance thing and we just had to show up to class. I didn't realize you meant we were supposed to take them. Can I still take them?

I'm slightly frustrated that I'm stuck taking basic math and English. I know how to ad stuff and how to read and write good, just put me through to med school already.

I feel like I need to drop from your math class to a lower-level class tomorrow. I was wondering if I still need to do tomorrow's homework for your class anyway.

I have been trying to register for classes for a couple of weeks and had no luck getting the computer to let me into my college account. I finally realized that I didn't finish my registration for college, so I wasn't actually even officially a student at the university yet. I got that fixed, and now it says I can register, but all of the classes are full. Would you happen to have room in yours?

I want you to know that I did the test review. Is it possible I show a zero on it because I didn't turn it in?

I just went onto the computer to take the online quiz and, it won't open for me. It said it was due yesterday. I didn't have a chance to take it by then, so I'm not sure why it won't let me take it now.

I have a 0% entered for the homework for chapter 3, and I don't know why. When you passed the homework back to us, I put mine in that stack that everyone else was taking their corrected homework out of.

Hi Professor Howard, I just went to the testing center, and they told me your test closed yesterday. I want you to know that it isn't my fault that I didn't know this. Those in my group told me you have announced the days it was open in class every day, but I had more important things to do than to attend class. So you see, it wasn't my fault that I didn't know because I wasn't in class when you told us. I was wondering when I can take it.

I wasn't in class on Friday, and there was an attendance quiz. How do I make up an attendance quiz for a day I wasn't in class?

Professor Howard, I was wondering if I could come in and get some help on number 7 on the practice test. I couldn't figure it out, so I guessed, and the length came up too short. I kept taking off a bit more and a bit more, but it still kept coming up short, so I think I need some help.

I have been struggling with the annuity project for my personal savings for retirement. Would it be possible to go over it in class? The numbers I am getting could pay off the national debt.

Always the Best Cheerleader

I just attended the funeral of a wonderful lady who died fairly young and very unexpectedly. If I could describe her in only a few words, I would have to say that Jana was the world's best cheerleader.

It's not that she was a cheerleader that stood on the side at games, holding pom-poms and dancing to excite the crowd. She was that kind of cheerleader when she was in high school, but she was much more than that.

The first time I met Jana was after we moved into our small rural community. It was summer, and the men were trying to put together a softball team. There weren't enough to field a whole team, so even though I was new to the area, I was asked to join.

I was quickly accepted by the others and enjoyed the comradery with the other men. One of those on our team was Jana's tall, strong, teenage son. But I didn't really meet Jana until our first game.

Jana came to that game to cheer for her son. She arrived early and procured for herself the seat behind the backstop, directly behind the batter's position. As fortune would have it, her cousin happened to be the pitcher for the opposing team. He was about twenty years older than she was, and he was also very competitive.

When Jana's son came up to bat, I quickly learned what kind of a cheerleader Jana could be. Her cousin pitched the ball, and the umpire called it a strike. Jana didn't agree.

"Hey, Ump," she called, "I have a coupon for a free eye exam that you can have. You apparently need it more than I do."

The umpire was used to her, and he didn't even flinch except for a slight smile. The second pitch arched high through the air and then dropped in at a steep angle.

"What are you trying to do with a pitch like that?" Jana hollered at her cousin. "Knock a jumbo jet out of the sky?"

"Shut up, Jana!" her cousin yelled.

"You shut up!" she yelled back.

The umpire just ignored them both and called another strike.

"Whoa! A strike?" Jana questioned. "Isn't there something about a wet ball being against the rules? That one probably came down soggy from floating through the clouds. It had to be worse than if somebody spits all over it."

Her son hit the next ball and made it to the base. Then I was up. Jana had to ask someone who I was, but she cheered for me and yelled at her cousin in my behalf just as she had for the others on our team. It didn't matter if she knew me or not. I was on her team. And after listening to her tell the umpire and her cousin off, I was glad that she was on the same side that I was.

Over the years, as I grew to know Jana better, I learned what a great cheerleader she was. She always arrived early to get the best seat, and then she cheered louder than anyone. It didn't matter if it was a state championship game for our high school or if it was the infrequent community competition of Daddy-Daughter Pig Wrestling. And each time the game was over, whether or not her team won, Jana was always the one who cheered the loudest.

But what was more important in our little community was that Jana was a cheerleader for the youth. She was there to encourage and help the young people through the tough times of their lives, not just in sports. Some of my own daughters, as teenagers, knew that Jana was a lady they could count on. She was always first to arrive when someone needed a friend.

So when Jana died suddenly, unexpectedly, and fairly young, I figured that she was just going early so she could claim a front row seat, allowing her to cheer for those she loved when they finished their game.

How to Lose a Cameraman

I saw my daughter alone in the crowd. "Where's the cameraman who was following you?"

She shrugged. "Lost, I guess." But her grin told me she knew more than she was letting on.

Some years ago, a movie company was doing a project called *Real Families, Real Answers* on ideas to help families stay strong. They wanted to film many different families in their normal day-to-day activities. We, with our ten children, were asked if we would participate.

My wife and I talked it over and visited with the producers. We knew we were not perfect parents, and we were afraid that the production would try to portray us as better than we truly were. Though we did not necessarily want the world to know all of our faults, we didn't want them to think we never made mistakes, either. They assured us that the project was to express mistakes as well as successes so that people could learn from both. With that assurance, we agreed.

They scheduled to be with us for four days. They would film everything we did. At noon on the appointed day, I met the film crew at their hotel room, and they followed me to our home. They spent the afternoon trying to help us adjust to having cameras all around us, telling us to just act natural.

That was not an easy adjustment. Although we had tried to prepare our children, there were many times when a camera came in their direction that they ran away.

"I'm sorry," I said. "We are just a little camera shy."

The producer nodded. "I have to admit that I haven't seen a family that is as nervous about cameras as yours is. But I think everyone will get used to it."

That that evening we had planned to go to Summerfest. Summerfest is when the local town closes off the main street and people bring crafts, garden produce, and all sorts of food to sell. There are games, contests, and lots of live music.

I told the camera crew that I didn't think it was a good idea to film there. "The people of our small town aren't used to such things," I said.

"Don't you worry about that," the producer replied. "We have filmed in cities all over the country, and nobody thinks twice about it."

I wasn't so sure, but we agreed to continue with the evening's plans. We arrived at Summerfest, and some of our older children, nervous at the thought of a camera following them in public, tried to make a break for it. But each cameraman chose someone to follow and stayed right on their tail.

My wife and I, with our smaller children, had a cameraman with us. As we moved into the street, people parted at the sight of the camera like the Red Sea parted before Moses. Everyone gave us a wide berth. Everywhere we went, the thick crowd quickly dispersed.

The producer said, "I've never seen anything like this. Why don't they just act natural?"

I laughed. "They are acting how they naturally do when they see a camera."

The cameraman filmed me winning the cow-milking contest. They filmed my daughter squealing all the way down a balloon slide after being nudged off the top by her sister. They filmed us eating sloppy barbecues and fresh corn on the cob and becoming a sticky mess. They filmed everything we did.

Meanwhile, my third-oldest daughter, who was in her late teens, had not been able to lose the cameraman who was following her. She had made many attempts, but all to no avail. She couldn't lose him in a crowd when everyone opened a path for him.

She had finally resigned herself to her fate when she stepped up to a booth selling huckleberry ice cream. The man running the booth leaned over and whispered to her, "Don't look now, but there is some strange man with a camera following you."

"What should I do?" my daughter whispered back.

"I don't know," the man said, "but he looks mighty suspicious."

"I have an idea," my daughter said, leaning closer. "You distract him, and I'll make a break for it."

And that, I found out, is how the cameraman got lost in the crowd.

A Little Bit of Oxygen

As I sat back into my seat on the plane, I looked at the brochure for the hotel where we would be staying. "Free Oxygen" it said in big, bold letters. I laughed to myself, thinking that that was a strange item to include on an amenity list.

We had flown from our five-thousand-foot altitude in Idaho to sea level at Lima, Peru. We spent quite a few days in that area enjoying the increased air pressure and feeling good. But then it was time to fly high up into the Andes, and our tour leaders suggested we prepare.

We discussed altitude sickness and its effect on people. Our team nurse suggested that we all take aspirin to thin our blood before we boarded the flight. My roommate, Steve, and I didn't have any, so we slipped off to a small corner store. When we asked for a bottle of aspirin, the confused clerk said, "Aspirin no come in bottle." She then produced aspirin in small cellophane packages at one sol (about thirty-three cents) a piece.

We took the appropriate dose, drank lots of water, and boarded the bus to the airport. Our ultimate destination was Pino, a city on Lake Titicaca. We were going to visit the floating islands on the lake and see much of the surrounding area.

Everyone chattered with anticipation, and finally our flight lifted off. It wasn't long before we could see the jagged peaks of the Andes through the plane's windows. As we flew, Steve, who had traveled much more than I had, explained to me the sensation of altitude sickness.

A few hours after our flight started, we landed at an airport at about thirteen thousand feet, and the plane taxied to the gate.

"How do you feel?" Steve asked.

"Fine," I said, thinking this was going to be easy.

"That's good," he laughed, "because they haven't decreased the cabin pressure and opened the doors."

Everyone talked and visited, each feeling they would be okay. But when the cabin pressure was decreased and the door opened, I suddenly gasped for air. I began to feel the strange sensation of the altitude sickness that Steve had told me about. It started with tingling in my toes, similar to when the blood is restricted to a limb of the body and then allowed to flow again. From the toes, the tingling started working its way up my leg. I had been told it would continue up through a person's body until it reached the head, and then the person would pass out. I started to quietly take deep breaths so as not to draw attention to myself, and the tingling faded away.

Everyone became a bit more serious, but we continued visiting as we made our way down the stairs that had been pushed up to the plane door. We were still disembarking when one of the women in our group, talking as she walked down the stairs, suddenly started speaking nonsensical words in somewhat slurred speech. A few men barely realized what was happening in time, and they were able to catch her as she fell to the tarmac.

Oxygen was brought, and within a short time she had regained consciousness and was lifted into a wheel-chair. By the time we had traveled the forty miles or so to our hotel, many members of our group had gone down. Oxygen was always rushed to the scene, and the person quickly recovered.

By dinnertime, we thought we were past the worst. As we ate, one member of our group leaned down toward his soup bowl. His wife was embarrassed. She nudged him.

"Dear, it's not polite to drink from your soup bowl in public." But when she nudged him, he slowly started to roll sideways. Those of us at a nearby table saw it and rushed to catch him on his way to the floor.

As he lay there, his eyes fluttered, and he started to sit up. He was encouraged to lie still until the oxygen arrived. He looked at us groggily and spoke sluggishly. "I had the strangest dream that I passed out."

You know, it's really nice when a hotel has free oxygen as one of its amenities.

Why Pigs Should Never Try to Fly

We were flying out of the Andes Mountains of Peru, heading for Lima. Our airplane looked like it had seen better days. Its airworthiness was somewhat questionable, and it wasn't very big. In addition, the airport runway didn't look like it was long enough even for a llama to get up to full speed, let alone an airplane, and at the end was a sheer drop.

But with assurance from our tour guides that all would be well, we boarded the plane. When we were ready, we were already cleared for take-off. We didn't have to wait for any other air traffic because there wasn't any.

As the plane built up speed, the rough runway jarred our teeth as we held onto our seats. It was with great relief that, just before we reached the sheer drop, the plane rose into the air.

As we settled back in our seats and tried to relax, Cliff smiled. "Well," he said, "that wasn't so bad. I've been in worse."

Cliff was the only one of our group who had been to Peru before. He had lived there for two years when he was younger. I turned to him. "Tell us about your other flights."

"Well, I can tell you that pigs should not try to fly," he laughed, and then he shared his story.

"I was at a small village high in the Andes," he said. "I needed to get to another village, and the fastest way was by air. Almost every village had some sort of airport. This one was no different. Along a mountain ridge, the villagers had terraced the hillside flat enough to create a runway.

"Fifteen of us boarded a small, single prop plane. Our plane started down the runway, but just as it was about to lift off, a pig decided it wanted to fly with us and ran out in front. Someone saw it coming and yelled for everyone to hold on. The pilot could do nothing but try to pull the plane up because we were going too fast, running out of runway, and approaching a quarter mile plunge.

"We picked up off the ground, but not enough to miss the pig. Our wheels hit him, and though they turned him into bacon, the impact tore our landing gear completely off. After we were airborne, the pilot circled so ground control, which consisted of a man in a shack with a two-way radio, could assess the damage. And even as he confirmed our situation, we could see our landing gear sitting in the dirt by the dead pig. The pilot knew he would have to make a belly landing and informed us that we were rerouting to the biggest airport in the area, the only one that had a fire department.

"At this point, the lady next to me started to scream. Her husband tried to calm her, but to no avail. She was yelling, 'If we crash and are killed, it will ruin my new alpaca sweater, and I paid nearly a thousand dollars for it!' If our situation hadn't been so desperate, I probably would have laughed.

"When we finally came to the airport we had rerouted to, we could see that their fire department consisted of one man in a rain slicker with a truck that had a cattle water tank full of water on the back. When we saw this, one man on our plane handed his friend a fifty-dollar bill. He said, 'I am paying you back the money I borrowed because I want to die with a clear conscience.'

"We all tucked ourselves up as ordered, and as we landed on the dirt runway, our plane acted like a plow, digging a long ditch. When we came to a stop, the friction had started the plane on fire, but the man with the water truck came and dumped the water into the ditch our plane had made, and that put the fire out."

"I bet the lady with the alpaca sweater was happy," I said.

Cliff laughed. "Actually, she said she was going to sue the fireman because her sweater got muddy after he dumped the water. And she said she was also going to wring the neck of every pig that she sees.

"And so you see," Cliff finished with a grin, "that is why pigs should never try to fly."

Fifteen Minutes of Fame

According to an old saying, everyone will have fifteen minutes of fame sometime in their life. When I was in high school, I hoped, with luck, to find mine in football.

Our high school offensive line coach was a great man, but he had a bit of a temper and lots of colorful language. He was also very strict in his discipline and in his expectations. If a player was ever responsible for a penalty, Coach pulled him out for a while.

Since no one liked to be pulled out, we all tried hard not to make mistakes. In addition, I had just met a new girl I liked, and I hoped to impress her. She couldn't make it to our first game, so she and her mother promised they would listen to the play-by-play broadcast on the radio.

In the third quarter of that hard-fought game, we had a very slim lead with the ball deep in our own territory. Our coach chose to go with a pass play. Our line held well, giving our backs plenty of time. Our quarterback made a great pass, and our receiver made a perfect catch and ran all the way for a touchdown.

But the play was called back. To my surprise, I was assessed a five-yard penalty for being too far down field. I was shocked because I felt I was simply making allowed blocks.

But Coach, true to form, pulled me out. During the next two plays, he lambasted me while our quarterback was sacked each time, dropping us back another fifteen yards. We were fourth down with thirty yards to go and less than ten yards out from the goal line behind us. By this point I was so mad I could hardly contain myself. I felt I hadn't really made a penalty, and then to have Coach yell at me was almost more than I could take.

Coach called a time-out and gathered us around. "Howard, what play requires the most out of you?" he asked.

I knew he already knew the answer, but I answered anyway. "A guard trap play."

"Why?" he asked.

"Because everything depends on me pulling out and cutting off any defensive men coming to the outside."

"That's right," Coach said. "And that is exactly the play we are going to run. And do you know why?"

"Why?" I asked.

"Because it will give you a chance to redeem yourself from your #@*& foolishness. The foolishness that cost us a touchdown. So, Howard, do you know what I expect?"

"What?" I asked.

"I expect a touchdown on this play," Coach replied. "Not just a #@*& first down and not just a nice run, but a touchdown. Is that understood?" I nodded, so he turned to the others and continued. "And if we don't get it, Howard will warm the bench by me for the rest of the season."

If I was mad before, I could hardly see straight now. The crowd was shocked when we lined up to run instead of to punt. When the ball was snapped, I pulled out and hit the cornerback so hard I laid him out flat. A linebacker came to stop the run, and I did the same to him. Our ball carrier was right behind me, and there was only one more defender. I took that defender out with a perfect down-field block, leaving our ball carrier with a free run all the way to the end zone.

As we came off of the field following the point after attempt, Coach grabbed me by the face mask. "Howard, you are the luckiest *#&@ in the world."

We won the game, and that touchdown play was the talk of the night. I hoped the girl I liked had heard it. The next day, I went to visit her. I asked her if the radio announcer had described my incredible play. She nodded enthusiastically.

"And we could hear your team's excitement because the radio announcer was right by them."

"Yeah," her grinning mother chimed in. "And we couldn't miss your other fifteen minutes of fame during the two previous plays as your coach described you to the world in the most colorful adjectives I have ever heard."

I just hope that, someday, I will get a shot at a better fifteen minutes of fame.

Halloween Revenge

I heard Lenny discussing plans with Butch and Buster for their annual attempt at playing a Halloween prank on Lenny's uncle, and I wondered how this one would turn out.

"We've got to make it so air will blow through them," Lenny said.

"How about we connect them inside the horn?" Butch suggested. "That will do it."

"Too obvious," Lenny replied. "Besides, he doesn't hit his horn enough. I would like to make it so they blow the whole time he's driving."

Lenny saw me and asked if I would like to join the three of them on their adventure. So far over the last few years, the score was Lenny's uncle three, and Lenny and his cohorts zero, so I declined.

"It's your loss," Lenny said. "We are going to get him good this year. By the way, do you have any idea of something on a pickup that would blow air constantly?"

"The only thing I can think of is the radiator fan," I replied.

"Howard, you're a genius," Lenny said.

I wondered what they were up to, but I was sure I would find out sooner or later.

Halloween night came, and Lenny, Butch, and Buster snuck into Lenny's uncle's yard. This year, the object of their attack was his pickup. Lenny stealthily led them in a wide arc around the house to avoid triggering any yard light. He had gone over there a few days earlier and mentally mapped out where everything was. Once around the house, they silently moved in on the pickup.

Buster stood guard, Butch positioned himself to relay needed items to Lenny, and Lenny climbed underneath the pickup to do the necessary work.

"Wire," Lenny whispered, reaching his hand out from under

the pickup. Butch dutifully handed the wire to him. "Pliers," Lenny said, sounding much like a doctor in surgery. Again, Butch handed the requested item. This continued until Lenny declared the job completed and slid out from under the pickup.

The three of them retraced their steps back in the direction they had come, and, for the first time in all of their attempted pranks on Lenny's uncle, they made it safely away.

The next day was Sunday, and when I went to church, I expected Lenny, Butch, and Buster to come banged, bruised, or missing hair like they had the previous years. But, instead, they were all smiles.

"How did the pranking go?" I asked.

"Perfect," Lenny said, pointing at his uncle's approaching pickup. "See for yourself."

I looked but couldn't see anything unusual about the pickup itself. But as it came closer, I noticed there was a large pack of dogs chasing it down the road. Dogs often chase vehicles, but this was far beyond reason. There were around twenty of them, and they ignored all other cars, intent in their pursuit. Lenny's uncle pulled into the church parking lot and stopped. The dogs all followed, howling. As Lenny's uncle stepped from his pickup, the dogs started growling, biting at his pickup tires, and lifting their legs and marking them.

"You stupid dogs!" Lenny's uncle yelled. "Get lost!"

He tried to shoo them away, but they quickly came back. He turned and saw Lenny standing there, grinning. Lenny's uncle marched right over to us and shook his finger in Lenny's face. "I know you had something to do with this, and as soon as I figure out what it is, you'll be sorry!"

Once Lenny's uncle left, I turned to Lenny. "What did you do?" I asked.

He laughed. "I wired silent dog whistles all along the bottom of his radiator. When he drives, he calls every dog in the neighborhood."

I guess it's now Lenny's uncle three, Lenny one.

The Floating Islands of Lake Titicaca

The group of faculty I was with toured lots of old ruins while traveling through Peru, but I much preferred the opportunities to actually see how the people lived. So the morning we were to go to the Floating Islands of Lake Titicaca, I was up early, ate breakfast, and then sat down to reread the material about the islands we had received. The literature told about the inhabitants' primitive lifestyle, and how, in the midst of our fast-paced world of technology, stepping onto the islands was like stepping into life as it was a few thousand years ago.

Lake Titicaca sits high in the Andes Mountains. Out group stayed in a city named Puno that was on the edge of the lake. The elevation there was more than twelve thousand feet, and many of our group were suffering from altitude sickness and had to stay at the hotel near oxygen. As the rest of the group gathered, I put aside my reading and excitedly prepared to step into this ancient culture.

We made our way to the dock where the boats we had chartered were tethered. We were not divided among the boats by numbers, but by weight, because each island could only bear a certain amount. The boat I was in soon pulled away from the dock and motored out into the open water, while the other boat went a different way to a different island. The water near the city was full of pollution, but as we traveled farther away, the water became cleaner and bluer.

We traveled for quite some time, and eventually we entered an area where the lake was shallow. This area was full of reeds, many with birds nesting in them. I wondered how a person could know where to go. When I asked the man who was driving the boat, he shrugged.

"I know the lake well," he said, "and I just drive to where

the island was last time I was there."

"What do you mean 'last time'?" I asked.

He laughed. "When a big wind comes up, even though the islands are anchored, they can move miles away. When that happens, I just go in the direction the wind was blowing until I find them."

When we finally pulled up to the island, I could hardly wait to step onto it. When I did, it was a singular sensation. It was like stepping onto a waterbed made of reeds. The feeling is hard to describe.

We looked at how they cooked food in clay cookstoves built to insulate the heat away from the reeds. They showed us how they made the islands from stacking reeds together. They also showed us how they added more reeds to the top of the island while the ones on the bottom gradually rotted away. Through an interpreter, they told us they lived mostly on fish and birds from the lake, along with money from tourists.

On this particular island there were five small reed huts, each about ten feet by ten feet in size. I asked if the island's occupants were all members of the same family. An old Peruvian shook his head. He said they got along better if they weren't related, so as children grew older, they would often find a different one to live on or start their own.

For a price, those living there would tell or show us anything we had an interest in, so I motioned that I would like to see what one of their huts looked like on the inside. One of the younger men held out his hand and said, in broken English, "For dollar." I pulled out a dollar and handed it to him, and he led me into his hut.

There were only two pieces of furniture in it. One was a small, two-person couch made of reeds. The other surprised me more than I can say. It was a good-sized television.

"Television?" I said in surprise. He grinned and nodded.

"But how?" I asked.

He motioned for me to follow him. We stepped outside, and he pointed to his roof. There, disguised by reeds, I saw a television antenna and a solar panel.

He slapped me on the back and proudly said, "This year, TV, next year, internet."

I had always wondered what technology was like a few thousand years ago.

Ancient and Modern Technology

Our faculty group had just finished touring the first of the floating islands of Lake Titicaca in Peru and had the rest of the day ahead of us to visit others. As we gathered back to our boat, some Peruvian men rowed up in a boat they had made from the same type of reeds that were used to build the floating islands. It was designed in the same Peruvian style as their ancestors had done for thousands of years. For only ten sol each (about $3.50), they offered to transport anyone around the lake to the other islands that we planned to visit.

Our whole group was fascinated by the boat and gathered around it. It was an incredible feat of ancient engineering with tightly interwoven reeds, even boasting a second story. It was rowed by two men who also steered it. When the men who owned it were ready to depart, only three of our group, myself included, decided to join them on that adventure.

"Are you really going to go on that thing?" Tom asked me.

"Of course I am," I replied.

"Aren't you afraid it will sink?" he asked.

I shook my head. "Not in the slightest."

He looked at me incredulously. "How can you be so sure?"

"The guys that built it are riding on it, and they don't have any qualms."

"Maybe so," Tom replied. "But I'll take modern technologies over ancient ones any day. I will travel in a modern boat, powered by a modern motor, and while I zip safely from island to island, you will be out there slowly going across the lake with little time to spend at each place."

But there was no way he could deter me. As a boy, I had been fascinated with the idea of building rafts. Of course, I must admit, everything I built sank almost immediately, but still the fascination lingered. To ride on something that actually floated and was made completely from reeds was a boyhood dream.

The three of us retrieved our life vests from the boat we had come in, paid our ten sol, and climbed aboard the reed boat. The two Peruvian men eased it away from the island and started rowing into the open lake.

Tom laughed and called out to me from the island. "See you at the bottom!"

I climbed the ladder to the second level and enjoyed the view and the swoosh swoosh of the paddles that kept us moving. It was much more peaceful than hearing the droning of a boat motor.

When we reached the next island, the rest of our group was nowhere to be seen. We had been quite a while, so we assumed they had come and gone. We enjoyed our tour of that island and then continued on to the next. We went to quite a few more islands, never seeing the rest of our group at any of them. Finally, we headed to our final destination where we were all to gather for the trip back to our hotel. Again, our group wasn't there.

We had a wonderful tour of that island and bought a few

souvenirs. It grew late, and still the others hadn't come, so we began to grow concerned that they had already been there and decided to head back to the hotel without us. We started to discuss how we might make our own way back when we heard the sputtering sound of a motorboat approaching. We looked, and sure enough, it was our group.

As they pulled up to the island, everyone in the boat was scowling. When they climbed out onto the island, Tom asked, "So how was your day?"

"Great!" I replied. I then told him about the peaceful excursion from island to island. "How about yours?"

"Our day," he replied with disgust, "was spent in the middle of the lake trying to get the stupid boat motor to start. We haven't been anywhere else since that first stop."

I grinned and said, "But aren't you glad you got to spend it with modern technology?"

A Tale of Two Soldiers

David and John were two men from the same small town who grew up on opposite sides of society. David was from the richest family in town. His family owned much of the land and some big companies, employing more than half of those who lived there. He didn't know what hard work was, having had everything he needed or wanted handed to him.

John's family was poor, and due to illness and medical costs, there was seldom enough to eat. As he grew older, in order to help out his family, he obtained a job on one of the farms that David's family owned. Every day after school, he changed into patched clothes and worked at backbreaking labor until after dark. He never had time for the fun activities most kids his age enjoyed.

David and John were in the same grade in school, and David viewed John with disdain. He mocked him and made his life miserable. More than once, in the depths of winter, David and his friends took John's threadbare coat, forcing him to endure the frigid temperature without it.

When they graduated, John was happy at the thought of being free of the insults and derision. But then World War II came, and both David and John were drafted into the army. To John's dismay, they ended up in the same platoon. Through basic training, John tried to avoid David as much as possible, but he was still forced to endure a lot of harassment from him and his friends.

As time went on, David became more and more popular. His family sent him many gifts from home, and David shared them throughout the platoon but never with John. John, on the other hand, received nothing more than the occasional letter from home.

Eventually, they were deployed to Europe. Their company saw a lot of action, and most thoughts turned to surviving. Then came the Battle of the Bulge, and the fighting intensified. Under a fierce bombardment, they were forced to fall back. As they did, a shell struck, killing some of David's squad and wounding him. The rest raced for cover, and David was left, wounded and dying, on the battlefield.

As he lay there with bullets whizzing past and shells falling all around, he was sure that one of his many friends would come to his rescue. Some time passed, and no one came. David had just about given up hope when he realized that someone was crawling toward him. The man worked under heavy fire to drag David back toward their line, and as he did, three times he was knocked down, twice from bullets and once by shrapnel from an explosion. But eventually he pulled David to safety, and as he did, he collapsed from loss of blood. That was when David finally got a look at who had saved him, and he gasped to see that it was John.

When David woke in the field hospital, he saw that he still had both arms and both legs. He asked the nurse about his condition and was told that he should make a full recovery. He then looked for John, and when he saw him, he noticed that he was missing a leg and had a horrible head wound. When David asked the nurse about John's condition, he was told his chance of survival wasn't very good.

He asked if his bed could be next to John's, and his request was granted. Though John lay there day after day, never moving, David talked to him and encouraged him. Then, one day, John briefly regained consciousness.

David asked, "John, why did you save my life, especially after how I treated you?"

John feebly answered, "I could never return home knowing I hadn't tried to rescue a brother." Those were the last words he ever spoke, for the next day he passed away.

When sometime later David became heir to a great fortune, he never forgot John. When people asked him why he spent his life and his fortune helping others, he simply said, "I could never return home knowing I hadn't tried to rescue a brother."

Of Love and Gratitude

Sally had been married for seven years, and all she wanted was to be a mother. Only a few months after she was married, she had prepared a nursery for the baby she dreamed of having.

But the years passed, and no baby came. She spent lots of money on doctors and specialists, but the final verdict was that she would never be able to have a baby. She had spent the last seven years praying for a child, and now that she felt God had abandoned her, she, in her bitterness, abandoned him.

She watched a news report of a young teenage mother who had a baby she didn't want and left it to die, and resentment began to grow in Sally's heart. How could God be so unjust? She knew she could have given that child the love her empty arms ached to give.

Feeling the way she did, Sally refused to attend her family's Thanksgiving gathering. In her heart she felt there was nothing left to be thankful for. Then, a few days after Thanksgiving, a knock came on her door. There stood a young woman who was obviously pregnant.

The young lady introduced herself as Amanda and said, "I'm expecting a baby next month, and I am trying to find a good mother for her. Different people I know gave me some names, and of those, I felt to come here."

"Why?" Sally asked.

"I know I can't take care of her the way she needs to be taken care of," Amanda said. "But I want to make sure the mother she goes to will love her like I do."

"And how are you going to do that?"

"If you will accept me into your home, I will see how you live and what you are like."

The thought passed through Sally's mind that this girl was

only trying to find a free place to live and that when the time came, she wouldn't actually give up her baby. She had heard of such things. Perhaps this girl would just rob them or even murder them in their sleep. Sally had so many bad thoughts, but she still found herself saying yes.

Sally set up a bedroom for Amanda and helped her settle in. When Sally's husband came home, he was surprised to find out about the new arrangement but agreed to it. As the days passed, Sally learned more about Amanda. She had grown up in a good home, but she had made some bad decisions. She had lived with the baby's father until he learned she was pregnant, and then he had thrown her out.

Social Services had worked out for a couple to adopt her baby, but she insisted on meeting them first. When she did, she felt they were not the ones she wanted to raise her daughter.

As the days grew into weeks, Sally found herself loving this wayward young woman. She realized that Amanda had a good heart and truly loved her baby. Sally wondered if Amanda would really be able to give her daughter up when it was time.

The day eventually came that Sally was rushing Amanda to the hospital. After many hours of hard labor, a sweet little girl was placed in Amanda's arms.

Amanda cried and said, "My sweet little angel, I have chosen a mother for you who will help you understand that I am not giving you up because I don't love you but because I do. I chose someone who will love you as I do but can give you the life I can't."

Amanda cuddled her little daughter close for some time, crying while she did, but finally, she handed the baby to Sally.

"What will you name her?" Amanda asked.

"I think I will name her 'Angel Amanda,'" Sally said.

And through the years, as Angel grew, Sally's heart was always full of gratitude, not only for the child she had received, but for the young woman who taught her what love really is.

Follow the Leader

It was the day before Thanksgiving, and we were on our way to the house of some relatives. It was a long way, and we had hoped to get off early. But, as things usually happen, we weren't able to leave until after noon. Thus it was late by the time we approached our destination.

We only had about thirty miles left to go when we saw the first detour sign. Then I saw the flashing lights of the highway department truck turn ahead of us and block the road. The truck had a big sign with an arrow that pointed in the direction of the detour. The road now closed ahead of us, we were the unlucky ones to be first turned down the detour route.

"If we would have just left fifteen minutes earlier," I grumbled, "we would have missed this."

As I followed the signs that directed us into the middle of the city, other cars followed our lead, and there were headlights behind us as far as I could see. The detour path was not well marked, and after we had approached the main street of the city, the signs disappeared completely. I presumed there could be different reasons for this. It could be the highway department ran out of signs, or it might be they decided that if they led us to another main road, we could find our own way from there. Of course, I considered, it might be they wanted us to experience the adventure of getting lost.

I made the decision to keep following the main street and watch for signs showing a route back to the interstate. It was almost midnight, so the city traffic was almost nonexistent, but the cars kept pouring in from the interstate. We went for about a mile at the slow city street speed, wondering if we would ever see a sign to get us back. Just then, the stoplight ahead of us turned red. We stopped, and the string of cars piled up behind us. By the time it turned green, there were scores of them.

We started on our way again, and the cars continued to follow us. We traveled another five miles, hitting quite a few more stop lights, and I had just started to wonder if this detour was simply some evil plan to keep us lost in the middle of this city forever when I spotted a sign indicating the way back to the interstate. At almost the same instant that I saw it, my wife saw a grocery store.

"That reminds me," she said, "we were supposed to bring some salad for the dinner tomorrow, and I never did get the things I needed."

I reluctantly turned onto the street by the store and then into the parking lot. That was when I realized I had an interesting situation. The cars behind me followed me onto the street and into the parking lot, too. As I parked, the driver of the first car behind me suddenly realized what I was doing and continued on out the other side of the parking lot, back onto Main Street, and disappeared in the direction of the interstate. All of the cars behind him followed his lead.

As I stepped from our van, I watched as car after car trailed its way through the parking lot. To get to the store, I had to dodge through them. I quickly made my way around the store, gathering the items on the list my wife had quickly scribbled out for me, and then went to pay for them.

But there were no clerks at the checkout. They were all standing by the window. One of them finally saw me and came to help.

"Sorry," he said. "There is something weird going on out in the parking lot. Hundreds of cars are driving through it."

I smiled. "Really? I wonder why they would be doing that."

When I went outside, the cars were still coming. I dodged between them again and climbed into my van. They were almost bumper to bumper, but finally I saw a short break and merged into the line of traffic, wondering about a very important question.

If I were to come back in the morning, would the line of cars still be driving through the grocery store parking lot?

A Really Lucky Day

When I lived in Buffalo, New York, in the early 1980s, some of us young men that were there made friends with an old bachelor. His last name was Hatzenbuler, so we all called him Hatz. He was the ultimate collector, and to me, his house was stacked from one end to the other with useless junk.

Since he was an organ builder by trade, he, of course, collected all sorts of musical things. He had just about every instrument known to mankind. He also had a baseball card collection, a stamp collection, an antique collection, and, most importantly to us young men, an old movie collection. The concept of video tapes was still in the future, so in order to watch a movie, a person had to either go to a theater or have his own movies and a projector. Hatz had literally hundreds of movies, and his house was stacked from one end to the other with canisters containing the reels.

On holidays, when we took a break from work, he invited us all to gather at his house and watch *Laurel and Hardy*, *The Keystone Cops*, or similar movies. Most of these were silent films, but Hatz was not just an organ builder; he also played expertly. He had built a small pipe organ in his house, and as we watched these old silent movies, he would accompany the film. Sometimes he would change things up by playing rock and roll to a horror film or scary music to a romantic one.

One Christmas, three other young men and I really had nowhere else to go, so Hatz invited the four of us to come to his house. We brought popcorn, chips, cookies, pop, and lots of other fun things to eat. Hatz's house, being the typical bachelor pad, we had to stack things up in order to have room to sit. But then we watched old silent movies until we were bleary-eyed and our stomachs hurt from laughing. As the evening rolled around, none of us felt like cooking, and we were tired of chips, so we decided to all go out to eat.

Before leaving, we decided to take a group picture. We all lined up in Hatz's hallway, and he set his camera on a big pile of scrapbooks. He set the timer on the camera and ran back to join us. We waited until we thought something must be wrong, and just as he moved to check the camera, it snapped a picture. It took three more such attempts before we finally waited long enough to actually get the desired shot.

About the only restaurant that was open for dinner on Christmas night was one of three that claimed to have been the first to introduce Buffalo chicken wings to the world. It had every kind of chicken wing from mild to incinerating, and we dared each other to eat hotter and hotter ones until we were nearly bleeding from our eyes with pain and our taste buds had been burned into oblivion. We laughed at each other, gasping in agony until we couldn't laugh anymore (definitely a guy thing). Then we headed back to Hatz's house.

But when we approached his front door, we immediately realized that something was wrong. The door frame was somewhat splintered, and the door was open. As we stepped into the front hallway, we immediately realized that Hatz's nice camera, the one we had used to take our picture, was gone. Hatz looked around and found nothing else missing.

"It's too bad about your camera," I said.

Hatz just grinned. "Actually, I'm very lucky that it was a dumb thief."

"What do you mean?" I asked.

"The camera was sitting on top of a stamp collection for which I have been offered twenty thousand dollars, and that was on top of my baseball card collection for which I was offered more than fifty thousand dollars. Yes, sir, it was definitely my lucky day to have such a stupid thief."

And I laughed, realizing that if it had been me, I, too, would have thought the camera was the only thing of value.

Even Santa Has Limitations

The community Christmas party was only a few days away when the woman in charge called and asked, "Daris, would you be willing to be Santa at our Christmas party this year?"

I taught the children music at church and knew them well. I love children and thought this would be a fun thing to do. I have also done a lot of acting and felt I could disguise my voice enough that they wouldn't recognize me, so I accepted.

The night came, and after the community dinner, I dressed in red garb, black boots, and fake beard and wig. At the appointed time, I ho-hoed my way into the big hall. The children rushed around me, and the adults had to clear a path so I could make my way to the chair that had been prepared for me.

The first child of the night was a rambunctious little boy who pushed his way to the front of the line. He had more energy than a category 5 hurricane and could be a challenging little boy, but I loved him.

I pulled him onto my lap. "So, Jason, have you been good this year?"

He nodded. "I've been the best ever."

I laughed my Santa laugh. "Oh, really? What about that time you didn't shut the gate on the horse corral and the whole community was out trying to round up the horses?"

His eyes grew wide with surprise. "You know about that?"

"Of course. Santa knows everything."

"Well," he said, "I've been mostly good most of the time."

I chuckled. "Don't worry about it. Even I'm not perfect. Did you know I accidentally let the reindeer out once? If you think chasing down horses is hard, you ought to see what it's like trying to corral flying reindeer."

He smiled and told me what he wanted for Christmas. I gave him a little hug and a bag of candy, and he climbed off of my lap and scampered off to his mother to tell her I was the real Santa.

I personalized each child's experience, and each one was surprised to find out how much I knew about them. A few of the older children were quite sure they knew who I was, but even they laughed at what I could tell them about themselves, and they were mostly there for the candy, anyway.

The last child of the night was a feisty little girl who was about six years old. She was the youngest in her family by quite a bit. I knew her well and knew that she hadn't waited to be last because she was shy. Quite the contrary. I could tell that she had something important on her mind.

I lifted her onto my lap and asked, "So, Brittany, have you been a good girl this year?"

She had heard me talk to the other children, and she paused. Finally she said, "Mostly. Sometimes I get mad when my brother teases me about being the baby of the family. And sometimes I don't do my chores."

I laughed. "Well, even I haven't been perfect."

"Really?" she asked.

"No," I replied. "I got mad at Rudolph one night when he was sneaking around scaring elves, jumping out at them with his glowing nose."

Her eyes grew wide with wonder. "Really?"

"Yes," I replied. "Even I can have one of those days, or nights, as it may be. So what would you like for Christmas?"

She sat up straight and looked right at me. "I want a baby brother so everyone will quit calling me the baby of the family."

Brittany's mom was there taking pictures, and she let out an exasperated gasp. "Brittany, I have told you and told you that you are not getting a baby brother!"

Brittany leaned up close and whispered in my ear. "You see how she is? I decided it was time to go over her head."

I laughed. "You know, Brittany, I'm not sure I'm over your mom's head on this one."

Yes, even Santa has limitations on what he can do.

Season of Miracles

My daughter called and asked if I would play Santa at her school arts program, so my wife, Donna, suggested that I just buy a Santa suit so that I could take on that role anytime I wanted. After we had purchased one, Donna asked me if she could post to her friends on Facebook that I would be willing to do it for others, and I told her she could.

Soon the requests poured in. Some were for family gatherings, and some were for big groups like elementary schools and church socials. The first person asked how much I charged, and when Donna asked me that question, I told her that charging would ruin the joy of it. I couldn't do a lot of them due to my time constraints, but what I could do, I would do for free.

Of all the requests that came, one interested me more than the others. A young lady named Tina wrote and requested that I come to the school for disabled adults where she worked.

She said, "The people here love Santa, but we haven't been able to get anyone to come for quite a few years. You won't have to have them sit on your lap or anything; just talk to them as you hand them bags of candy."

I had associated with some of these wonderful people, and hoping that I could brighten their lives, I felt like it would be a worthwhile place to go. Donna made the necessary arrangements, and on the appointed day, she drove us to the school while I slipped into my costume. All week I had had dozens of children, teenagers, and even adults climb on my lap, so I asked Donna about what Tina had said and if there was a rule against the students at the school doing that as well.

She shrugged and said, "There must be."

After we had arrived, Donna checked my costume for any last-minute adjustments, and then I was ready to go. Tina announced to the group that there was a special guest, and then I ho-hoed and jingled my way into the room. One student, who was about fifty years old, started to cry.

"I haven't seen Santa in forever," she said.

She started running to me, but the workers helped her wait until it was her turn.

Tina stayed close by me to tell me a little about each student and to take pictures. I picked up the first candy bag and read the name. The student made her way to the front and shyly accepted her gift. The second student was a large lady who was about forty years old. After I read her name, she walked briskly to me and plopped on my lap. All of the workers gasped. I asked Tina if that was against the rules.

"No," she said, "we just thought they might hurt you."

I laughed. "I am a former state champion wrestler. I can handle it."

The employees all relaxed as student after student came to the front, sat on my lap, and received their gifts. Most of them hugged me and told me they loved me. I hugged them back and said I loved them, too.

Finally, the last lady, almost totally paralyzed, was wheeled up in a wheelchair. Tina whispered that this lady, who was about fifty years old, could hardly move and could make almost no sounds at all. I set the bag of candy on her lap then reached out and took her hand. When I did, she lightly squeezed mine and spoke in a slow but clear voice.

"Thank . . . you . . . Santa."

Tina gasped, and everyone in the room cheered. Tina looked at me and started to cry as she said, "I guess it truly is a season of miracles. She has never spoken since her accident ten years ago."

As I left, I thought that the biggest miracle of all was actually the one in my heart, because these people helped me remember what Christmas is really all about.

New Year's Motivation

At the start of the new year, I was determined to lose weight. I worked out every morning for quite a while and barely saw the weight drop. But I could tell I was putting on more muscle. Then, as usually happens, there came a week when I was burning the candle at both ends, and trying to squeeze out one more minute for exercise was impossible.

After missing one week, it was easier to exercise fewer days the next week, and fewer the next, and soon I had given up altogether. Every once in a while I would give a half-hearted try at restarting, but it never lasted.

Then came Christmastime. With all of the candies, cookies, and cakes, I watched my weight start to climb again. The calves that I raise can gain a couple of pounds per day, and I told my wife that I could best them any day of the week.

It was also during this holiday season that I made the determination to visit people I hadn't seen in some time. One couple, the Masters, had lived in our community for many years. When they did, I had visited them quite often. But I hadn't seen them for over a year because they had moved into an assisted living center.

I drove the twenty miles to town through the falling snow. I went inside the living center and found the main hall packed with at least a hundred people. Probably every resident was there, and most of them had family visiting. I decided that I would just say a brief hello to the Masters and come back another day.

I asked the young lady at the information desk if she knew where they were. She pointed to a small table in the center of the room. Mr. and Mrs. Masters were sitting alone playing checkers. As I turned toward them, the young lady called after me.

"A couple of things you will want to know. Mr. Masters is nearly blind and almost totally deaf, so you will have to speak loudly."

I thanked her and made my way over to their table.

"Hi," I said to them. "Do you remember me?"

"What?" Mr. Masters said in a voice that echoed across the room, causing everyone else in the hall to grow quiet.

"It's me, Daris Howard," I shouted at the same volume, feeling embarrassed as everyone turned to look at me. "So how's life?"

"My wife is right there," Mr. Masters said, pointing across the table.

People around the room started to giggle as I yelled louder.

"So, do you like living here?"

"No, thanks," Mr. Masters said. "We don't drink beer. But you can if you want."

I don't drink alcohol, but I decided it wasn't worth belaboring the point, so I tried another subject. "Do you have good food?" I yelled.

"Of course I'm in a good mood," Mr. Masters yelled back. "It's Christmastime."

I decided to give it one more try. As loud as I could, I asked, "So how's life treating you?"

"Well, of course not," Mr. Masters said indignantly. "Whatever gave you the idea that my wife was beating me? I never lose at checkers."

I just shook my head and sighed. "Happy holidays," I said as I turned to leave.

I had only gone about ten feet when I heard Mr. Masters yell to his wife, "Who did he say he was?"

"That's Daris Howard," she yelled back.

He must have been used to her voice tone because he

immediately understood. He shook his head.

"You've got to be kidding!" he yelled. "Wow! He has gotten fat! It must be all of the beer he's drinking."

As everyone in the hall burst into laughter, I hurried outside to my car with a renewed dedication to restart my exercise program.

A Theater and a Memory

I was in a theater recently, performing in a production of *A Christmas Carol*, when an interesting memory returned to me.

When I was a teenager, the theater didn't have live performances but ran inexpensive movies. I loved movies, but a movie isn't much fun to attend alone, and unfortunately, I was so shy that it was hard for me to ask any girl out on a date. In addition, I was responsible for much of the work on my father's farm and seldom had time.

But a new movie called *Star Wars* was showing, and I knew I just had to see it. All of my friends had, and when they started quoting lines or talking about the plot, I would leave so they wouldn't spoil it for me.

I couldn't afford to go to the fancy theater where it first ran, so I had to wait for it to come to the cheaper one. In addition, when it first came to town, we were in the middle of harvest, and I was working from before daylight until way after dark.

But a year after the movie first ran, it came around again and was at this inexpensive theater. There was a girl named Mary that I liked, and I mustered all my courage and called her. She accepted my date invitation, and my heart soared.

On the appointed Saturday, I worked hard and fast all day until I was exhausted. I milked the cows and worked through my evening chores as quickly as I could and then showered and dressed in my best clothes. My heart pounded, and I could hardly breathe as I drove to Mary's house.

I walked to the door and rang the bell. Mary's mother answered, and when I asked for Mary, she said, "Mary isn't here. She's gone on a date."

I guess the look on my face must have said a lot because she seemed to realize something wasn't quite right and quickly added, "But I'll make sure she knows you dropped by."

I walked back to my car, feeling like I had just crash-landed on earth. I wondered if I should go to the movie or just go back home. I knew I wouldn't have the courage to ask someone on a date for a long time, and that I might never get to see the show again, but it wasn't fun anymore.

Finally, I decided to go anyway. I drove to the theater and bought a ticket and some popcorn. It seemed everywhere I turned I ran into friends with their dates, and they each asked me who I came with. I always changed the subject instead of answering. Eventually, I was able to slip into the theater where I was less noticeable in the dim light.

This theater did have one interesting feature that I knew about. In the balcony, there was a solitary seat in a corner by itself, and I quickly claimed it for my own.

I enjoyed the movie, though sitting alone wasn't much fun, and seeing couples together everywhere made me jealous. I was also exhausted from the day's work and struggled to stay awake. When the show was over, I stayed in my seat until the theater was almost empty so I wouldn't bump into any more of my friends. But when I walked into the foyer, I ran right into one of my best friends. His date was none other than Mary. I think, by the look on her face, that until that moment she had forgotten I had even asked her out. But when she tried later to convince me to try again, I never could.

So, as I waited at rehearsal for my turn on stage, remembering that night long ago, I went into the balcony and sat in the solitary seat, grateful those dating years were behind me.

Applying for a New Job

I was working on my graduate degree in mathematics and was struggling to support my little family when I saw an ad in the local paper. A vocational school was searching for a part-time math teacher. I thought about how much fun it would be to teach students math applicable to their chosen areas of study, so I drove to the school and filled out an application.

A few days later the secretary called and asked me to come in for an interview. I arrived early and was directed to a lounge where I could wait with the other applicants. Jobs were somewhat scarce, and my heart sank as I saw the large number of people who had applied. As a group, we were ushered into a large conference room where all of the school's teachers and administrators were waiting.

After we were seated, the school's director addressed us.

"Just so you understand, we are not looking for a math teacher because we necessarily feel our students need to learn math, but because the state recently informed us that they are going to require all of our students to have at least a basic proficiency in it or they will cut our funding. To be honest, there are some here who feel that a math class is a big waste of valuable teaching time."

"You can say that again," one of the teachers said.

"David," the director replied turning to the teacher who had spoken, "since you obviously have a strong opinion on the subject, why don't you go ahead and express it?"

"I teach auto body," David said. "Can any of you give me one good use of mathematics for a student who works on cars? No, you can't, and let me tell you why. There isn't one. My students should be spending their time learning how to detail and perfect the way a car looks, not wasting their time doing useless math."

"Now wait just a minute!" another man said. "Yes, I teach

engineering, and indeed we use a lot of math, but I use it in simple things, too, even in something like balancing my checkbook."

David rolled his eyes. "I've heard it all before. Blah, blah, blah, you can't live without it. Well, let me tell you, I'm no math genius, and I do just fine."

Many other opinions were expressed, with some of the discussion becoming quite heated. I learned that the spectrum ran from those like David who felt his students didn't need it at all, to Bill, the engineering teacher, who wanted his students to have all the math they could. I also learned that they wanted this discussion out in the open so those of us applying for the job would understand the sentiments of those in the school and not be surprised.

"Well, we have to do it," the school director said. "So what room can we use?"

"How about my classroom," David said with what I felt was a bit of a smirk. "It is the biggest and nicest classroom in the school."

"Thank you, David," the director replied. "Knowing how you feel on the subject, it's nice of you to offer."

David grinned. "It's my pleasure. Besides, if my students are doing math, I won't be using it."

When that meeting ended, the director and a smaller group of teachers, including David and Bill, interviewed each applicant individually. That was when I learned that the administration only wanted to pay for one class, even though they expected the math diversity to range from simple addition for some to logarithms and complex numbers for others.

The next morning, the secretary called and said I had the job if I wanted it. I felt proud to think that I was chosen from among all of the applicants. I prepared all morning and went later that day to teach my first class. That was when I found out why David had volunteered his classroom. He moved a car from across the shop to right by where I was teaching, and while his students were with me, he sanded the car, ground on it, and did whatever else he could to make noise. Bill dropped by to see how it was going. Yelling over the din, I told him I felt honored they had chosen me.

He laughed and patted me on the back. "Don't get too big of a head over it. After the discussion yesterday, every single one of the other applicants withdrew their applications."

And as I tried to teach over the sanding and pounding, I wondered if they, perhaps, were smarter than I was.

An Expensive Lesson

I had taken on the job of teaching math to all of the students at a vocational school. Unfortunately, I was assigned to the auto-body classroom, and the auto-body teacher stated that "Learning math is a stupid waste of time." He moved a car near the classroom, and while his students were with me, he did whatever he could to make noise so that I had to yell to be heard by a person right next to me.

Many of the auto-body students picked up their teacher's attitude and skipped my class, using that time to smoke. The star auto body student, Steven, instead chose to come to my class in order to harass me. He would sit with his feet on the desk, swear at me, and call other students fools if they tried to learn any math.

I had to teach math ranging from addition all the way to logarithms, so on the first day, I organized the students into groups based on their field of study and their abilities. Then I had them work on problems I had designed for them specifically related to their work. I would rotate between the groups, helping them and getting them started on another problem before moving on to another group.

I tried to be friendly and work with everyone, especially Steven, but he was determined that there was nothing he could learn from me. The more I tried to be friends with him, the more obnoxious he became. I must admit that I was happy the day I learned he had finished his program and would be heading off to work.

But he decided to come to my class one last time to tell everyone that he had a job where he didn't need math and that the other students were fools for listening to a &#%! idiot teacher like me. At that point, I showed him the door, and he left, swearing at me on his way out.

Things were better after that, except for trying to teach over the noise. But then, after about a month, Steven was back. I asked him if he wanted something. He said no, but he sat quietly with his feet on the floor. In addition, one student asked for help, and I started to yell as usual to be heard when I suddenly realized the sanding and grinding noises weren't there. After I excused the class, Steven stayed, waiting until everyone else was gone.

He then came to me and humbly asked, "Will you teach me some math?"

"Why would you want me to do that?" I asked.

"Well," he said, "at the shop where I work, I am considered an independent contractor, and I price a job, do the work, and collect the payment. From that payment I pay all of the parts and other costs, and I also make sure the shop gets twenty percent. My first job was a very expensive car worth hundreds of thousands of dollars. I knew how to look up the parts and price them, but I didn't know how to add, and I definitely didn't know how to take a percentage, so I just guessed."

"How much were you off?" I asked.

Steven looked down, extremely embarrassed, as he answered. "The cost of the parts alone was more than twenty-five thousand dollars, and I guessed the total for everything to be only fifteen thousand dollars."

I gasped. "You were ten thousand dollars short of making your expenses?"

He nodded. "I will have to work for about four more months for free just to pay it off."

I laid out a practice problem for him and showed him how to add the values and take the percentage using a calculator. We did a few more problems, and I had him double check everything. When we finished, he smiled. "That's not so hard."

I asked him if he would share with our class how he used math, but he said he was too embarrassed. But he did tell me he made sure his teacher knew.

The next day I was surprised to see the auto body students who always went out to smoke being herded into my classroom by their teacher. He threatened to kick them out of the program if they didn't learn their math. In addition, he stayed and learned with them.

After the rest of the class left, he came up to me and said, "After all, a person can always use math."

Food or Naught

My sweet Aunt Bea was a strong-willed, determined woman. She was also kind, loving, and willing to help anyone in need. In addition, she grew up during the Great Depression, and like most people who lived during that challenging time, she couldn't stand to see anything go to waste.

She lived alone, and one Monday evening I decided to take my family to visit her. When we arrived, she was busily pulling weeds in her garden.

When she saw us, she smiled and wiped the sweat from her face.

"Well, I'll be," she said. "I just knew someone would come, so I made extra food. Come in and have something to eat."

I laughed. Aunt Bea always made extra food. I had never been to her house and not had her want to feed me. She loved to cook, and everything she made was incredibly good.

"We're okay, Aunt Bea," I said. "We just had dinner."

"I'm sure you can at least eat a bite of cake," she replied. "I have some that is a couple of days old, and I don't want it to go to waste."

I knew that we weren't going to get away without having some, so I said, "How about we give you a hand with your garden first?"

She nodded. "That would be nice."

We helped weed her garden, and when we finished, we all went into the house and had some wonderful chocolate cake and some cold milk. We also enjoyed a great visit. As we were leaving, she wrapped up the last of the cake and handed it to me. "I don't want to throw this out. You take this with you so it all gets used up."

I thanked her, we all hugged her, and then we headed on our way. Only a couple of weeks later, I learned that Aunt Bea had fallen and was in the hospital. As I was trying to find out what had happened and what hospital she was in, I learned that one of my paramedic friends had responded to the call.

"Can you tell me what happened?" I asked him.

"As far as we could tell," David replied, "she was out working in her garden when she tripped over a garden hose, fell, and broke her hip. That was at about eight o'clock at night. No one was around to help her, so she scooted along on the ground all the way to the house. It took her until one o' clock in the morning to get into the kitchen, where she pulled the phone down off of the counter and dialed 9-1-1."

"That must have been horribly painful for her," I said.

"That is true," David replied. "But you won't believe what she did when we came. While we were trying to prepare her so we could lift her onto the stretcher, she asked us if she would be in the hospital for a long time. When we told her that it looked as though her hip was broken and that she would likely have an extended stay there, she insisted that we needed to slow down. We paused, knowing she was in a lot of pain, thinking she wanted us to be more careful so she wouldn't hurt as much."

"That's understandable," I said.

"But that's not what she wanted at all," David replied. "She said she had a nice lasagna in the fridge and some cake on the counter. She wanted us to stop and eat them. When we insisted that we needed to get her to the hospital, she said, 'It's really good lasagna. And the chocolate cake is nice and fresh.'"

"So did you have some?" I asked.

David laughed. "Are you kidding? She refused to let us take her until we finally agreed to at least take the cake with us so it wouldn't go to waste."

A Strange Football Lesson

Our high school quarterback, Rand, picked himself up off of the ground and yelled at us linemen. "Can't you guys do your job and keep them out? I've already been sacked twice!"

"That's why they call him a quarterback," Lenny whispered to me. "He's only got a quarter of a brain. He doesn't know where the blame lies."

I didn't have a chance to respond because at that moment, Coach Smith, our line coach, called a time-out. As we ran over and formed a huddle at the sideline, he grabbed Rand by the face mask.

"Who the *&#% do you think you are?" he hollered. "I heard you yelling at my linemen, and it wasn't their fault. I timed how long they kept the defense out, and it was more than fifteen seconds. That's more than two to three times as long as you should need. What were you doing back in that pocket, taking a nap?"

Rand was obviously angry at the rebuke. Coach Smith usually only yelled at us linemen, and the back coach dealt with the backs.

"No," Rand countered. "But no one was open."

"You take that up with the receivers," Coach said. "If you have a problem with my linemen, you talk to me. But if you yell at them again, you'll wish you hadn't."

As we ran back onto the field, Rand was mumbling. "Who does he think he is? He's not the back coach, and he can't tell me what to do."

We soon made a first down, and, as if to test Coach Smith, Rand called a pass on the next play. We again kept out the defense for almost fifteen seconds before Rand finally grounded the ball just as he was being smashed into the turf. As he climbed to his feet, he looked at Coach Smith as if daring him to do anything and then he yelled at us again.

Coach Smith immediately called me over. "Howard, tell the others that on the next play you all are to move aside and let the other team plow that arrogant &#*% into the dirt."

I gasped. "But Coach, we've never done anything like that before."

"He's got a lesson to learn. You let them through, or I'll put someone in who will. And you keep doing it until I tell you otherwise."

I nodded and hurried back to the huddle. I told the other linemen what he said. They turned to look at him in disbelief, and he nodded his assurance. So on the next play, we did what went totally against our natures. We moved aside and let the opposing team nearly dig a grave with our quarterback.

The crowd gasped. Rand stayed down, and a referee time-out was called. The back coach called us over. "What the &#*% do you think you're doing?" he yelled.

Coach Smith answered for us. "Until that worthless fool realizes what a great job they are doing protecting him, and he apologizes, my linemen will continue to let him defend himself."

Rand came off of the field, and a replacement came on. After a couple of plays, we had another first down, and Rand came back in. The first thing he did was berate us for what had happened.

"My coach told me what Coach Smith said, but if you think I'm going to apologize, you can forget it. You better do your job, or you're the ones who will be hurtin'."

"It ain't hurtin' us," Lenny said with a grin as we turned and saw Coach Smith angrily signal for us to let the other team through again. When the ball was snapped, and we moved aside, Rand turned to run but was quickly buried by the defense. This time the back coach called a timeout. He pulled everyone together.

"Rand," he said, "I do believe you owe your teammates an

apology. You take care of it and quit yelling at them, or I will replace you for the rest of the game."

Rand mumbled an apology, to which Coach Smith said, "I can't hear you." After a couple more tries, Coach Smith felt it was sufficient.

As we went back in, Lenny said, "I'm glad Rand finally apologized. I was beginning to fear we'd be planning his funeral."

Valentine's Day Questions

My roommate, John, drove the rest of us crazy. He was always burning something when he cooked, and most of the time he just cooked beans. In addition, his diet of beans made him a veritable methane volcano, continually spewing forth toxic gas.

Whether it was cooking, destroying the bathroom, or just generally messing up the apartment, he had a masterful talent akin to the god of chaos. But John had one big thing going for him that I definitely didn't have. He was really good looking. Not that I thought he was, but the girls sure did. They swooned around him so much that it made a person sick, or, in my case, maybe a bit jealous, especially with Valentine's Day coming up.

Valentine's Day was on a Saturday, and that was the day of the girl's preference dance. Since it wasn't common for a girl to ask a guy out in those days, the preference dance was the one time they could show a guy that they really liked him by being the one to initiate the invite.

The campus population was fifty-six percent female, so statistically, every guy had a good chance. There were a few girls I liked, and I really hoped one of them would ask me. Of course, all nine of us guys in the apartment had similar hopes, so in mid-January we created an apartment pool as to who would be asked first, second, third, etc. No one except John put him first on the list, and no one except myself put me as last. Many of my roommates thought that since I was a varsity athlete, I would be asked first.

I, however, knew that wrestling didn't draw a great crowd of female admirers, and I was rather shy. My forays into dating were quite limited. But what was humiliating to the rest of us was that John had six invites before any of the rest of us even had one. But, finally, everyone in our apartment had received one except me. I won the apartment pool, consisting of two gallons of ice cream, but that was little consolation as we approached the Monday before the dance and I still hadn't been asked. John started to rub it in until my other roommates, understanding how I felt, threatened his life.

There was one girl, more than all of the others, I hoped to go out with. Her name was Bonnie, and she was the only girl in my Fortran programming class. She was beautiful with long dark hair and big brown eyes. There were more than fifty other guys in the class, but she happened to sit by me. Besides herself, I was the best programmer, and she liked to check her work against mine.

I decided I would ask her out, but I didn't dare ask her for Saturday, sure she would have already asked someone to preference. I thought maybe I would ask her to a movie for a different day. On that Monday I mustered all of my courage as I went to class.

Just before class started, I turned to her and said, "Uh, Bonnie, I was wondering if you . . ." I didn't get a chance to finish asking because just then the teacher slammed his books on his desk and spoke in an angry tone.

"It has come to my knowledge that a few of you young men have asked our student secretary out and then tried to get her to give you advance copies of my tests! She has been honest and never even tried to look at them herself, and let me tell you that asking her out for that reason is the height of rudeness. If it happens again, I will personally take care of the matter. It would be best if none of you to ask her out while you are my students."

I knew that Bonnie was the department student secretary. I hadn't had any such thoughts in mind, but now I knew I couldn't ask her for fear she might think that was what I wanted. My heart sank. When the teacher finished his angry discourse, she turned to me.

"Was there something you wanted to ask?"

I felt so discouraged I couldn't even look her in the eye as I shrugged and answered, "No."

Each evening as my roommates talked about their fun plans for Saturday, I left the apartment so I wouldn't have to listen.

As programming class ended Tuesday, Bonnie asked, "Are you excited about the dance on Saturday?"

I just shrugged. She looked at me with surprise.

"Aren't you going?"

I shook my head.

"Haven't you been asked?"

Again I shook my head.

On Wednesday, Bonnie handed me a program. "Would you mind going through my code and checking my output?"

"I'd be happy to," I said. "When do you need it back?"

"I hate to put any pressure on you, but I kind of need it by tomorrow," she said.

"Okay," I replied. "I'll get it done."

After class, I went to my apartment, but all of my roommates were talking about their fun plans for Saturday, so I went to the library to study so I wouldn't have to listen. I did all of my homework, and then I pulled out Bonnie's program. I traced through the logic of the program. I quickly realized the output was spelling something. Still, it didn't dawn on me that it was more than a normal program until I realized it had spelled my name. I quickly worked through the rest and found the output to be, "Daris, will you go with me to the preference dance on Saturday?"

I almost cried as I quickly put together a program in return that simply output, "Yes!"

I had a lot of fun being with Bonnie that night. And since she invited me first, I didn't feel any reservation asking her out after that. And to this day, when I look at computer code, I will remember what was one of the most creative dance invites I ever have.

Gasping for Air

Coach blew his whistle, which brought us to a stop. His favorite conditioning exercise was to have us run on our hands and knees back and forth across the wrestling room. He started us off by blowing his whistle and ended the exercise in the same way. In between, we were supposed to run as many laps back and forth as possible. It was exhausting, especially after having already practiced for a couple of hours.

"One more time," Coach called after about thirty seconds of rest.

He blew his whistle again, and off we raced. In order not to skin our knees, we ran in what we called a bear run. Back and forth we went, hoping for the whistle to blow. Finally it did, and we dropped to the mat.

"How many did you get, Howard?" Kevin, our 185-pound wrestler, asked.

"Ten," I answered.

"Ten?" he said, rolling his eyes. "What, are you trying to be the bear-run champion?"

"How many did you get?" I asked.

"Three," Kevin replied. "And that is more than plenty."

"One more time," Coach called, feeling we had had enough rest.

"But you've said one more time for the past five times," Kevin said.

"I didn't say it would be the last time," Coach replied. "I just said do it one more time."

Coach then blew the whistle. Only a few of us took off at full speed, while most of the others only loped.

As the weeks progressed, most of the team didn't take this

part of the conditioning seriously. While the same few of us pushed as hard as we could, the others only did it halfheartedly—if they did it at all. Kevin was the worst. He would find some way to slip out for a drink, or flop on the mat, or claim an injury.

At the first of the season, it didn't end up being too bad for him. The opponents we opened the season with weren't too tough, and Kevin, as good as he was, pinned each of them in the first or second round.

But then came the first night that Kevin faced an opponent who was able to fight his way out of the pinning holds Kevin tried on him. Though Kevin was ahead by six points at the end of the second round, he was gasping for air, and his lips were blue.

Kevin was in the top position in the third round, and his opponent quickly dropped to his knees on the mat. Kevin moved slowly, taking every second possible trying to catch his breath. He was finally ready, and the ref blew the whistle. Instantly, Kevin's opponent did a reversal and was on top. Kevin's lead was cut to four. Kevin should have been able to defend against that, but he was moving too slowly. Kevin's opponent started plowing him into the mat, positioning him for a pin.

Suddenly, Kevin hollered, "My eye! My eye! I think I jammed my contact in my eye."

The ref stopped the match and looked into Kevin's eye. "I don't see a contact," he said.

"Oh, no!" Kevin said. "I've lost it." He immediately dropped to his knees and started searching. The ref signaled to Coach, and Coach called us all out to help. We moved our hands carefully across the mat but found nothing.

As the rest of us were heading back to the bench so the match could resume, I whispered to Kevin, "I didn't know you wore contacts."

"I don't," he replied.

I then realized he had just done it as a diversion to catch his breath, and though he was able to hold on and win by two points, I was disgusted.

"So are you going to take conditioning more seriously?" I asked.

"I doubt it," he replied. "But I might take up wearing contacts."

An Honest Swim Check

February is scout month, and that always brings back lots of memories of my years as scoutmaster to eighteen boys. When I became scoutmaster, I promised the boys I would work with them on any good thing that they wanted to do. They soon learned, however, that there were things I wasn't fond of. Swimming was one of them.

When I had to complete the scoutmaster swim certification, I thought I was going to drown, and so did the boys. That was why we hadn't even arrived at scout camp before Gordy started teasing me about passing the swim check.

"Are you even going to try?" he asked me as we neared the camp.

"I'm not only going to try," I replied, "I'm going to do it."

"We only have one week up here," Gordy said. "Don't you need something like six months just to get in shape?"

"Ha, ha," I replied. "Maybe I will pass mine off before you do yours."

I knew Gordy disliked swimming more than any other boy in our troop, so it seemed crazy that he was the one teasing me.

"Actually, I don't even plan to do my swim check," Gordy said.

"But I thought you wanted to work on the canoeing merit badge," I replied. "You have to pass your swim check before you can do anything else on the lake."

"I'm paying Seth to do my swim check for me," he said.

"No one else is going to do your swim for you," I replied. "First, it isn't honest, and second, you need to prove that you can save yourself if something happens."

I started trying to speak to Seth about it, but the boys

reminded me that he was in the pickup his dad was driving.

"Well, when we get to camp," I told them, "remind me to talk to him."

We arrived at scout camp just after six o'clock in the morning. The sun was just coming up as we started the arduous task of hauling all of our gear to our campsite. My boys preferred solitude, and we had reserved the campsite farthest away from everything.

By seven o'clock, all of our gear was packed in. We decided to set up camp later because it was time for the swim check. We put on our swimsuits and headed to the lake. Although it was July, the water flowing into the lake from melting snow still had a glimmer of ice along the edge. The thought of jumping in stole my breath away even before I took the plunge.

We had to swim four times from dock to dock. I was struggling by the time I finished the second lap, and by the time I finished the third, I could sense the end of my life nearing, both from freezing to death and from lack of oxygen. Both Gordy and I gave up at about the same time.

"We'll try again later," I said, trying to encourage him.

We went and set up camp, and after we were rested, I turned to Gordy. "Let's go give that swim check another try."

Gordy groaned. "Why can't I just have Seth do it for me?"

"Because you will feel so much better doing it honestly," I replied.

"Not likely," he growled.

We headed down to the lake, and all of the other boys followed to cheer us on— or, more likely, to make fun of us. We approached the board containing our swim tags, and I couldn't find mine. I hunted and hunted for it, but it wasn't there. Then one of the boys found it—not just on the swim check board, but on the swim expert board.

Just then, Seth's dad walked up, rubbing his hair dry with a towel.

"Hey, Daris," he said. "I hope you don't mind, but I wanted to swim, and since I didn't have my physical on file, they wouldn't let me. So I just told them I was you. They made me pass the swim check first, so you are all set."

Gordy smirked. "Nothing like doing it honestly."

I arrived early to prepare for the night's play. Our family was running summer theatre in the small town where we lived, and it was the opening night of our first production. I was working to get everything set up before the cast and audience members arrived when Sid, our oldest thespian, walked in.

I had grown accustomed to Sid coming early. He seemed to like the extra time to tell me stories while I worked, and I enjoyed it as well. The city had started tearing down the building next door, and that seemed to stir his memory.

"I remember one night," Sid said, "that I was out in front of that building they are tearing down. I was the lookout for a little bit of nighttime activity, and we barely avoided getting into trouble."

That piqued my curiosity. "What kind of nighttime activity, and what kind of trouble?" I asked.

"Well, I was just a boy," Sid said. "It was during the Prohibition, and there was a group of men who would gather to drink and gamble. Of course, both activities were illegal, so I was hired to be the lookout. I was around nine or ten years old, and they paid me a dollar a night. That was a lot of money back then."

"There was drinking and gambling here during the Prohibition?" I asked.

"You can bet your life on it," Sid said.

"So what kind of trouble was there?" I asked.

"The men had gathered in the basement of that building," Sid said, "and I was outside doing my job when a couple of police officers approached. I gave the preassigned signal and then hid. The police officers came to the building and forced their way in. When they reappeared, they hadn't arrested anyone. I knew there was no other way out, so after the policemen left, I found a way into the building and made my way downstairs. The room was empty, and I wondered where the men could have gone.

"I watched the building for most of the night, thinking they had hidden somewhere inside and eventually had to come out, but no one ever did. This happened more than once and in more than one building. Eventually, one of the men told me that there were hidden tunnels running under the streets between the buildings. I went into those rooms and searched for the tunnels, but I never found them. I guess the tunnels' secrets died with those men years ago."

After that, we had to finish getting ready for the show since the rest of the cast members and the first customers were arriving.

The summer wore on, and then one night, shortly after I arrived to start the night's preparations, Sid excitedly came in.

"Come see what I saw!"

We went outside and over to the building they were tearing down. They had demolished it and had used a backhoe to load the debris into dump trucks all day. Though the perimeter around the building was fenced, Sid found a small opening, and we climbed down into the exposed basement. In one cinder block wall, there was a small hole. We pulled on what looked like a block and discovered a door made to blend in with the rest of the wall.

Behind the door we found an opening that was only waist high, and we had to get on our hands and knees to crawl into it. It was obviously a tunnel going underneath the street, and in the tunnel we found some old liquor bottles and a few scattered poker cards.

As we climbed back out and dusted ourselves off, Sid grinned. "I'm glad I eventually learned the secret, and I'm glad you could be here with me."

Although Sid has since passed away and the tunnel was hidden when the foundation of the new building was poured, the story will live on with me.

A Calf Named Lucky

It was mid-February in the middle of my junior year in high school, and the temperature was about twenty degrees below zero. I went to take care of the pregnant cows, and Buttercup, who was past due, was nowhere to be found. Instead, there was a hole in the fence, and beyond it were hoof prints in the two-foot-deep snow. The full moon shining off of the snow made tracking her easy. A slight melt followed by a freeze had made a snow crust hard enough for me to walk on the top.

Buttercup's trail led a half mile east and then crisscrossed. As I debated which way to go, I heard a coyote howl. Unlike a wolf, which is large and to which an unarmed man would have little defense, a coyote is much smaller, and I could probably stand up to two or three of them. However, when they call to each other, they are usually forming a pack. A pack can be very dangerous since some will distract their prey while the others attack from behind.

I counted responses to the first call: one, two, three, four. I quit counting and looked for a means of defense. I saw some trees in the moonlight and moved toward them to find a branch I could use as a club. But when I reached the trees, I found another problem. Buttercup was there with her calf, which was still wet and likely only minutes old. I realized that it wasn't me the coyotes were smelling, but the blood from the calf's birth. The calf couldn't walk yet, and though Buttercup might be able to fight for herself, she couldn't while defending her calf.

I knew that if I left the calf, it would surely be killed. Buttercup might be killed, too, trying to defend it. But if I tried to carry the calf to the barn, the pack would likely overtake us, jeopardizing my life as well. I looked at the baby, small, wet, and shivering, and I knew I couldn't leave him. I lifted him over one shoulder and picked up a stick in the other hand. I was grateful wrestling season had barely ended, so I was still in good shape, but as I stepped onto the snow, carrying eighty extra pounds, the top crust broke and I sank in past my knees.

I counted on the coyote pack coming to clean up the blood and placenta from the birth first and hoped that would buy me a five-to-ten minute head start, but I didn't plan on the snow slowing me down. I trudged forward, moving as fast as I could, with Buttercup falling in behind me on the path I broke for us.

The pack closed in quickly on the place we left. I could hear the coyotes fighting over what they found as I pushed myself hard, feeling the freezing air burning my lungs. The sweat started pouring down my back, freezing in ice ribbons the length of my body. I had traveled about a quarter mile when I heard a coyote howl and knew they were back on our trail.

The adrenaline surged through me, and though I was exhausted, I quickened my pace. I was almost to the edge of where the cow herd had tramped the snow, where I would be able to walk easier, when the first coyotes attacked Buttercup. She whirled to fight, and I dropped the calf to join her. A coyote darted in and bit at the calf, and I swung my stick and missed the coyote. I was too exhausted to fight, but I had little choice. But suddenly I didn't have to. The other cows, hearing the calf cry from the coyote bite, and naturally hating dogs, smelled the coyotes and came to chase them away. After a moment's rest, with what little strength I could muster, I carried the calf to the barn.

Before I made it to the house, my dad was there searching for me. I was shivering so badly he rushed me inside and helped me pull off my winter clothes while my mother heated a cup of milk. For the next two weeks I fought pneumonia and a fever.

When I was finally up again, though I was still weak, my dad patted my shoulder and said, "There is something you need to see."

I followed him to the barn, and there was the cutest little calf. As it nuzzled me, my dad said, "We named him Lucky, but you can change his name if you want to."

I smiled. "I think Lucky pretty much sums it up."

A Wild Goose Chase

When I came home, my oldest daughter came to meet me. "Daddy, you have to do something about the geese. They think they're dogs, and they chased us when we came home from school today."

The previous year, my children had thought it would be fun to have a whole menagerie of animals. They especially wanted chickens so they could gather eggs. We looked through the poultry catalog together and ordered a mixture of baby chicks, ducklings, and a couple of geese. We raised them through the spring, and by late summer our chickens were laying eggs, our ducks were swimming up and down the ditch, and our geese thought they were dogs.

The problem was that when we got the birds, the geese were too bossy and didn't get along with the chicks or the ducks. We ended up having to put the geese in the yard with our new puppy. But the puppy did what puppies do. He started chasing cars, and the geese followed suit. When someone passed our yard or home to visit, he barked at them. The geese, of course, picked this up and started honking at people. However, their honking sounded more like barking. They drank milk and ate dog food out of the dog dish, turned their noses up at grain, and chased the cats.

It was cute when they were small and fluffy, and the cats ignored them, but they didn't stay that way very long. Soon the geese were grown, and it wasn't funny anymore. Dog food costs more than grain, the cats grew afraid of them, and the geese became bossier, even barking at us.

But the day I came home and learned that they had threatened my children, I knew the geese had to go. I didn't want to kill them, so I let everyone in our community know that I had a couple of free geese that thought they were dogs. It wasn't too long before a middle-aged couple, who lived a couple of miles away called and said they would like them. They lived on a corner of a country road that few people traveled, and they felt the geese would be happy there.

My next job was to catch the geese. I went outside, and the geese came after me. I thought that would make them easy to catch. But when I didn't run from them like my children did, they suddenly didn't want to chase me anymore. The tables were turned, and they ran. It was definitely the proverbial wild goose chase. I fell in the ditch, ripped my pants on a fence, and slid on some dog and goose poop on the lawn. But I finally got one cornered, and when it tried to rush past me, I tackled it.

Seeing his mate in trouble, the second goose came after me, flapping his wings and barking. At the last minute, since I didn't flee, he turned to run, but it was too late for him. I held his mate with one arm and grabbed him with the other. I stuffed them, fighting and scratching, into a couple of gunny sacks.

My neighbors locked the geese in their barn for a couple of days, feeding them dog food and getting them used to the fact that this was their new home. A couple of weeks passed, and I asked my neighbor how he liked the geese. He said he loved them. After their run-in with me, the geese no longer chased people, but their car chasing intensified.

"There are only a couple of things I don't like," he said. "First, they chase my cat. And second, after word got out about our watchdog geese, our quiet road has become quite the thoroughfare. There is a constant stream of traffic coming to see our barking geese chase cars."

I decided to check it out for myself, so I drove down his road, watching for the birds. As I approached the corner where my neighbors live, I couldn't see the geese anywhere. Then, suddenly, they came rushing out after me. They had been waiting in ambush, one behind an old pickup and the other, on the opposite side of the road, behind a lilac bush.

They chased me down the road, and then they went back home to terrorize the cat and eat their dog food.

Water Problems

It was the end-of-summer meeting for our community theater board. My family ran a summer theatre, and my wife and I had come to pay the rent we owed and participate in the discussion on upcoming events.

The old theater had seen a lot of activity over the years. It had opened in the days of vaudeville and had been converted to cinemas when the first movies came out. But as newer theaters in neighboring towns had been built, it had lost its profitability and closed its doors. The city had come in possession of it for unpaid taxes, and a volunteer board had been formed to try to repair it and keep it open.

The summer theatre that my family ran helped pay for quite a bit of the expense incurred in heating and maintaining the building. Our board also worked to host any event we could that would bring in additional revenue.

As the meeting was wrapping up, the board president turned to me. "Daris, could you put up the advertisement on the marquee for the play that the visiting group is bringing?"

"Sure," I replied.

After the meeting, while my wife was chatting with some of the other board members, I hauled the big ladder and box of letters outside and changed the sign. The old marquee was a big source of revenue for the theater. When we didn't have any productions going on, we rented it out for twenty dollars per day for any ad or message someone wanted to post. I had put up everything from political announcements to wedding proposals.

I finished the advertisement for the play that was coming the next weekend, and my wife and I went home. A couple of days later, our local paper ran a story saying that our small town was in a flurry of activity over concern that something was wrong with the water. There had been a run on bottled water at the town grocery store and gas stations. The manager at the grocery store said they were bringing in extra truckloads of bottled water to meet the demand.

The reporter said he had not had a chance to talk with town officials to find out what the problem was, but the circulating rumor was that the federal government might be shutting off the city water over the weekend. This concerned me because we needed water in the theater for the visiting theatre production.

The next day, the paper said the town officials claimed the rumors of water problems were completely false, and no one should panic. The third day, the paper came out with an article saying that, despite the town official's assurances that all was okay, the run on the water was continuing. The town officials said they were determined to find the source of where the rumor started.

That evening I received a call from a town official. "Mr. Howard," he said, "we have traced the concerns about the city water to the theater. Did anyone report getting sick or anything during your plays this summer?"

"No," I replied.

"Well, we are going to have to run some tests. If there is a problem, we will have to close it down."

"But there is a visiting group bringing a play this weekend," I replied.

"I'm afraid that public safety is more important," he said. "I've asked the city engineer to meet me there in a half hour. Can you join us?"

I told him I would be there and reluctantly made the drive. I arrived there at almost the same time as the town official. The engineer was already there, and he was staring at the marquee. "What is that?" he said, pointing at the sign.

"It's is a play a visiting group is bringing this weekend," I replied.

"Well, I think I see our problem," he told us.

As the town official and I both looked up, we knew he was right.

"I'll adjust it," I said.

So I added "Drama:" in front of the play info I had put up the week before, which read, "Don't Drink the Water, August 18-19."

Beatrice first saw Merritt when she went to eighth grade. Actually, he had been there during all of her years going to school, but two things had changed: her and him. He was now tall and handsome, and, well, she was at an age where boys were more interesting to her.

She started flirting with him. But boys are an interesting lot, and he being a typical one didn't get it. He seemed far more interested in work, sports, and horses. But toward the end of their high school years, he finally noticed her.

After they had both graduated, they started dating. Merritt was the antithesis of Beatrice. She was vibrant, talkative, and the life of the party. Merritt was much quieter and more thoughtful. But he was a good man, and despite their differences, Beatrice knew she was falling for him.

Unfortunately, good paying jobs were hard to find, so Merritt decided he needed to go where the work: California. Beatrice hoped to convince him to stay home, but Merritt was determined to make his own way in life. Merritt lined up a job and found a cheap apartment with other young men of the same age.

It was a sad parting for Beatrice when she waved goodbye to him at the train station, and it didn't take her long afterward to know that she didn't want them to be apart. Beatrice wasn't anything if she wasn't tenacious, so she asked her family for help. Her uncle worked to get her some free train tickets, and a cousin found her a temporary job and a place to stay.

It wasn't long before Beatrice's train pulled into California. Merritt was happy to see her, and their relationship grew as they spent all of their free time together. But the months passed quickly, and Beatrice's temporary job was ending. She would soon need to head back home, and Merritt was not giving any indication of taking their relationship to the next level. When she hinted at marriage, he took her to get a marriage license to alleviate her worry.

Merritt, meanwhile, began to get cold feet. He loved her, but World War II was raging, and life was far from settled. He was concerned about his ability to take care of himself and a new bride. The wedding license would expire on March 31st, and Beatrice could see that day approaching quickly. She determined that if nothing happened, she would be on a train home by April 1st.

Merritt suggested that she should go home while he worked for a while longer. Then, when she came back, they would get married. She said that if he wanted her to go home, she would, but she would not be coming back. With that, she left to pack her belongings.

It took that for Merritt to realize how much he loved her and didn't want to lose her. But it was already late in the evening of March 31st, so he went to her, and they hurried to the home of the ecclesiastical leader of their local church. Though it was late, this wonderful man invited them in and performed the wedding with his family as witnesses.

But then Merritt and Beatrice didn't know what to do. It was already past midnight, and they had no plans, so they decided to go to their separate apartments and get together after work the next day to try to figure out how to move forward with their marriage.

The next morning, when Merritt awoke and prepared to go to work, he had to endure the typical April Fools' Day pranks from his roommates. When one of them asked him why he didn't pull any of his own, he answered in his normal, quiet way.

"Well, I guess it's because the only thing I can think about is the fact that I got married last night."

His roommates roared with laughter. "Merritt," one of them said, "you'll have to try something a little more believable if you are going to pull a joke on us."

A Strange Story

Edward approached me at the end of our last class and asked if we could visit privately in my office. Once there, he asked if he could have more time to finish the last assignments.

"I have worked hard," he said, "but I got married about a month ago, and it has been hard to keep my mind on school work."

"Let me check your grades," I replied

I checked his grades, and he had indeed been doing okay until the last month. I decided to grant his request and let him finish up the last of the course work. We filled out the appropriate form and marked for him to have one year, the maximum time allowed.

He returned to his home, and as the year progressed, I emailed him a couple of times but received no response. As the due date approached, I sent him a final reminder, but still heard nothing. Then, a month after the deadline, he wrote and asked if he could still complete the course. I reminded him that university policy wouldn't accept the makeup work beyond the year already given.

Another month went by, and I received an email from a woman who said she was Edward's wife. She told me Edward had suddenly passed away and the only thing standing between him and his degree was a passing grade in my class. She requested that I give him the passing grade so he could have that honor and she could mention it at his funeral.

Of course I was skeptical wondering if it was just an unusual way to get the grade. However, I have been teaching for a long time and have learned that often, the stranger a story, the truer it is. But I needed to independently verify what I had been told, so I took his information to our secretary. I explained what had transpired and asked her to search the online obituaries from the area where Edward lived to see if she could find anything.

She was skeptical, but later that day she came to my office.

"Look what I found," she said, as she handed me a paper.

There in front of me was an obituary, including a picture of Edward. I felt bad that I had doubted his wife, but I felt even worse that he had passed away so young. As far as the request, I didn't know what to do. The ultimate decision wasn't mine to make.

I started by visiting with my department chairwoman. She didn't know what to do and had me call and visit with the college dean. He didn't know what to do, so he went with me to visit with the academic vice president.

"You want to give a grade that a student didn't earn?" the academic vice president asked incredulously.

I explained the situation, and then he asked, as each person before him had, "Are you sure the young man really passed away?" I showed him the obituary. He shook his head in disbelief. "I have never seen such a strange coincidence of events."

He then turned to the college dean. "What do you think?"

"Well," the college dean said, "the young man had done most of the class work and came just short of passing. And it's not like anyone is going to question his understanding of the material at some place of employment. In addition, we give honorary degrees, and aren't they, in a way, honor for classes people haven't taken? That is all this is, really, an honorary degree."

The academic vice president thought about it for a brief moment. Finally, he nodded. "Daris, you fill out the paperwork and get it to me, and I will sign it."

I worked hard over the next couple of days to get everything in place since the funeral was fast approaching. It had taken me most of a week, but I finally had the required signatures and was able to get the grade changed at the registrar's office.

I wrote to Edward's wife to tell her the news, and it wasn't long before I received her reply.

"Thanks anyway, but the local university decided to grant him credit in that class and already gave him an honorary degree."

Making Connection

As our flight came to a stop, my wife, Donna, quickly used her smartphone to find where our next flight would be. "It's at gate eighty," she told me.

"That's lucky," I said. "We're at seventy-three. That should mean it's right next door."

I will be the first to admit that I am not a world-class traveler. I seldom get out of Idaho. But Donna had always dreamed of us going to Hawaii, so when we hit our thirtieth anniversary, we decided to start saving money. It took over a year and lots of scrimping, but by searching for the very best deals, we were finally on our way.

We wanted to get to Hawaii as early in the day as possible so we could get settled in, but when it was time for our first flight's departure, there wasn't even a plane at the gate.

An airline representative spoke over the intercom and said, "For those on Flight 1437 to Los Angeles, there has been a slight delay. The flight coming out of California took off an hour late, and those on Flight 1437 will be taking that same plane back. Anyone who has less than an hour between connections will need to come to the kiosk so we can rebook your next flight."

Donna went to set things up for us, and when she came back, she was quite upset. The new flight was four hours later than our original one. Not only would we have to sit in the airport for those four hours, but we wouldn't get to Hawaii until after dark. The airline representative said that our only other option would be to run for our connection when we landed and hope for the best.

When we finally boarded our first flight, it was a small regional jet, and our carry-on suitcases wouldn't fit in the overhead bins, so we had to check them at the jet gate. We knew this would add to our dilemma because we would have to get them back before we could even attempt to meet the next flight.

By the time we landed, it was already time for our next flight to leave, so once Donna had found our next gate number, and the plane was parked, we had settled on a plan. Donna would run for the next plane and see if she could stall them. I would keep our two personal items and grab our suitcases.

"But that is way too much for you to carry," Donna said.

I just laughed. "With the gates only being seven numbers apart, it's probably almost next door. Besides, you'll need to be able to run unhindered." She nodded and ran off up the jetway.

After forever, our suitcases finally arrived, and with the two personal items slung around my neck, I grabbed one suitcase in each hand and headed up the jetway ramp into the airport. An airline representative was there waiting for me.

"Your wife made it to the next gate, and they will wait for you, but only if you hurry."

At that instant, over the intercom came the announcement, "Passenger Daris Howard, your flight is ready to leave; please report to gate eighty."

I took off running in the direction the airline worker pointed, and I could see a sign almost one-hundred yards ahead pointing left, with eighty among the gate numbers. I thought I just had to get to that corner and I would be there. Arriving at that point, my heart pounding faster than an Indy 500 car's pistons, I saw each gate was about forty yards apart, and with my gate seventh among them, it was over a quarter mile.

Determined to try, I took off running again. With only about fifty yards left, I finally had to slow to an exhausted scamper.

Just then, the intercom boomed, "Last call for passenger Daris Howard."

Donna saw me, told them, and hurried to take a suitcase.

The airline people held the door until I could collapse through it. I fell into a chair, gasping, wishing one of the oxygen masks would fall from the ceiling

"I think I've just run halfway to Hawaii," I said. "I wonder whose sadistic idea it was to make gates that are only seven numbers apart over a half mile away."

One of the other passengers heard me and laughed. "Welcome to the world of airline travel."

A Big, Tough Heart

Milton spoke strongly to his family. "We will not stop for anything except another equipment breakdown!"

Milton was a tough, old farmer, known for a no-nonsense attitude and for running a tight ship, and that spring hadn't started out well. Just when it was time to start planting potatoes, the rains came and threw everything a couple of weeks behind. In addition, they were having a lot of mechanical trouble. Their equipment was getting old, and they had only begun planting potatoes when the chain on the planter broke. It took almost an hour to fix it. They started again but hadn't made even one time up the field when one of the furrowers snapped. That didn't take too long to fix, but they had again just started when one of the tires on the planter went flat.

Milton's children knew the best thing to do at this point was to just try avoiding their dad. He was in a sour mood. The oldest son, David, was happy to have the assignment of taking the tire to the repair shop. That kept him away from his father for a short time.

Though it wasn't close to noon yet, Milton told everyone to get some lunch and be prepared to work steadily until after dark because once they got going they weren't going to stop. Everyone scattered before he could change his mind. But as soon as David brought the tire back, everyone was summoned, and the planting began again.

They planted for a while and then went back to load the planter. They had just started when the belt on the machine filling the planter popped loose.

Milton was not about to let it stop them. He turned to David. "Get the potato fork and start filling the planter by hand while I get the tools to fix the belt."

Thinking of the back-breaking work forking potatoes was

almost more than David could bear, but he was not about to argue. He shoveled until the sweat poured down his face, and he finished about the same time Milton completed the repair on the belt.

They were soon planting again, but it wasn't long before something else broke down. That was how things went all day. They would make some progress only to have something else break, and though Milton was keeping his frustration under control, everyone could tell that he was reaching the boiling point.

When it came time for dinner, he told everyone to grab a bite to eat whenever they could because they weren't stopping. They continued on through the evening, and as the sun was just going down, Milton suddenly brought the equipment to a halt. An audible groan could be heard from everyone, sure that there was another breakdown. Milton wouldn't stop for anything else.

Milton yelled to David, "Get me a shovel!"

The only thing David could think of that required a shovel was the potatoes getting jammed up in the planter mechanism. He was sure it would be his own miserable job to dig them out. He ran across the field to the pickup, grabbed a shovel, and ran back.

Milton took the shovel and walked around in front of the tractor. When he did, a mother and father killdeer, birds that nest on the ground, started going crazy, trying to draw him away. But Milton was undeterred.

Then everyone watched something they would never forget. This rough, old farmer scooped up the little killdeer nest onto the shovel and carried it over to the ditch bank at the end of the field. He gently set the nest down, came back to his tractor, and climbed aboard. Away they went again at a furious pace.

Everyone there smiled in disbelief because, for the first time in their lives, they had seen something besides a breakdown that Milton would stop for.

A Really Smart Horse

My dad and my brothers always told me that our old horse, Annie, was likely the smartest horse in the world. My brothers even joked that she might be smarter than some people. But it wasn't until the first time my dad sent me on Annie to cut a cow from the herd that I began to understand what they were talking about.

My dad had been a cowboy in his early years, winning many awards as a bronc rider. He had also done some horse racing. He was almost thirty-three years old when he married, and he decided he should make some changes. He determined that rodeo was not the life for a family man, nor the direction he wanted for his sons, so he gave it up. He only kept a couple of his best horses and sold the rest. By the time I came into the picture, Annie was the only horse left.

"She is not only smart," my dad said, "but she is quick at figuring out what needs to be done."

On one particular day, one of our cows, Crook Nose, escaped from the barn without being milked. Dad had tried to stop her by shutting the gate, but old Crook Nose slammed into it, smashing Dad against the wall.

Dad was bruised and furious. He set me astride old Annie. "Go get the runaway bucket of hamburger before I turn her into stew meat."

"But Dad," I said, "I've never cut a cow from the herd before."

"Don't worry about that," Dad said. "It's not your job to cut the cow away from the others; it's Annie's. All you have to do is show her which cow it is. Then let her have her lead and hang on for dear life."

I definitely knew I could show her which cow it was. I was

only seven years old, but I had started riding with my dad when I was three and was riding alone by the time I was five.

Annie and I galloped to the pasture, and when I saw the right cow, I turned Annie toward her. I could tell when Annie got her sights fixed on Crook Nose because she started chasing without me having to direct her.

But I didn't follow my dad's instructions as I should have. Oh, I did give Annie her rein, and I thought I was holding on well. But at one point, when we were chasing the cow at full speed through an area of sagebrush, the cow turned left around a low bush and Annie followed. I didn't. I flew off of Annie's back, crashing to the ground.

Luckily, we had passed the lava rock and were on the edge of the grassy pasture. In addition, the sagebrush was a young plant and was soft enough that it broke my fall.

By the time I had pulled myself together, Annie had dutifully chased the cow clear back to the barn. Once dad had the cow locked into a stall, he looked out, saw me walking back, and knew I would survive, so he went back to milking.

My brothers had seen the riderless horse bring the cow back to the barn and were waiting for me when I arrived.

They all laughed when one of them said, "See what we mean about Annie being smarter than some humans? She didn't need you to tell her how to bring a cow back to the barn."

I nodded. "I know. After all, I've seen each of you walking back before."

A Brilliant Student

David was an incredibly brilliant student, but sometimes that was his downfall. For example, my students were supposed to write a program called Twenty-One where two players would take turns removing from one to three items out of twenty-one. The goal was to force your opponent to remove the last one.

We were programming on an old Unix system through terminals. The graphics were ugly, and the interface was limited. All I asked them to do was a fairly simple input and an output of how many items were left at each step. But David couldn't stop there. He created a program with images that I hadn't even dreamed was possible on a terminal display. It showed twenty-one little robots and one big one. Once a person chose a number, the big robot would turn and shoot that many little robots.

The only problem with all of this was that while David was programming it, the assignment became two weeks overdue, and we had already had two more. When he showed it to me, I was astounded. I couldn't really flunk him with his incredible talent, but I didn't know how to grade him on the things that he missed. I scolded him a bit about not doing the work assigned, but I couldn't doubt his ability.

One day David signed onto a bulletin board where engineers and computer scientists were discussing an unsolved problem that had been around for about ten years. David added his thoughts about a certain way it might be done. The group moderator came unglued, telling David he was new to the group and didn't know what he was talking about. He asked David his age, and when David responded that he was eighteen, the moderator went berserk. He called David all sorts of mean things, insisting that the problem was unsolvable and a computer program for it could not be written.

David didn't get ruffled at all. Instead, he worked on the

problem and brought it to me. I went through it with him and found his work to be incredible. I only found a few slight math errors, which we fixed. With that, he said he was going to code it.

"But David," I said, "even if this program can be written, the intensity of it is almost overwhelming."

"That's what makes it fun," he replied. "But there is one problem. If I put all of my time into this, I'm not sure I can pass your class."

I thought about it and then said, "David, I really should expect you to do the assignments in my class, but if you can program this, I promise I will pass you."

He smiled and left to go to work. I didn't see him for about four weeks, and when he came back, he looked like he hadn't slept since we last spoke. But he was smiling and happy. He held up a paper.

"I did it."

"Did you share your work with the programming group on the bulletin board?" I asked.

He nodded. "That's what this paper is. It's their feedback. Here, read it."

I read the comments from the other programmers who had tested his code, and though they found minor errors, David had done what many had said was impossible. They were all amazed. But the best comment was the one from the moderator.

It said, "To Mr. David Patterson: We would like to offer you a job with our company, and my boss told me to propose a starting wage at four times the normal rate—this wage is double mine, and I have worked here for more than twenty years. In addition, I have been told that if I don't apologize, I will lose my job. I truly am sorry for the inappropriate things I said, and I hope you will forgive me and consider employment with us."

When I finished reading it, David smiled at me. "Well, do I pass the class?"

I laughed. "I think you can safely assume you passed."

A Life-Changing Decision

One of the soldiers turned to Private Howard. "What about you, Old Man? Want to join us to find some beautiful island girls when we get to Hawaii?"

As they approached Hawaii, all the soldiers could talk about was the fun they would have when they got there. World War II was raging, and for months they had been enduring the hardships of boot camp. They enjoyed a short leave after finishing, and now they were being shipped out to Hawaii before heading to the fighting in the Pacific. But as they traveled, Private Merrill Howard sat quietly, not joining in the excitement of the others.

He had grown up in a farm family, and when his father became ill, Merrill dropped out of school to help. He worked all day, and then studied by candlelight, trying to keep up with his school work. Once in a while he would take a day and go back to school to test on the lessons he had prepared. When graduation came, those in his class were shocked to learn that he had finished the course work on his own and would be graduating with them.

He had hoped to go to college but had barely enrolled when his father asked him to return home again. He was twenty-five when Japan attacked Pearl Harbor, and he wasn't married, so it wasn't long before his draft number came up. Now, as the others chattered excitedly, all he could think about was the commitment he had made to himself to do the things he had been taught and to always attend church when he could.

So, to the other soldier's question, Private Howard shook his head. "Since it will be Sunday when we get there, I'm hoping to go to church."

The other soldier and those near roared with laughter.

"You've got to be kidding," one of them said. "You know that soon you could be dead, and you have a chance to live it up for a few days. You're not going to waste time going to church, are you?"

Word of what Private Howard had said spread quickly, and soon everyone was teasing him. It made the final part of the journey seem to last forever.

When they arrived in Hawaii, Private Howard wondered how he would get to church. But they hadn't even had time to settle in when a young lieutenant showed up at their barracks.

"Anyone in this company want to attend church?" he asked.

The other soldiers pointed at Private Howard and chortled.

"You want to go to church?" the lieutenant asked him. Private Howard nodded, so the lieutenant led him out to a waiting truck. A few men joined them from other units, all telling the same story of being teased for going.

While most of the soldiers spent their time in riotous living, Private Howard and those few men with him spent the week enjoying church socials. But soon the week was over, and everyone packed their duffle bags.

As Private Howard lined up with the others, his commander barked at him, "Howard, take your gear with you and report to the officer's hall."

When Private Howard arrived at the hall, he found the other men he had gone to church with already there. The lieutenant was also there.

When Private Howard walked in, the lieutenant said, "You men are to be transported to the computer center at Diamond Head. You will be working there for the duration of your service. The general over that computing command center told me to find some good men to work there. I could think of no better way than by finding out who would stick to what he knew was right by attending church, even when he was far from home."

Now, on Memorial Day, when I look at the flag flying over my father's grave, indicating his service to his country, I am proud that Private Howard is my father. I'm also grateful that his example taught me to do what I know is right, even when I'm far from home.

Calculating Mischief

I was a junior in high school when the first calculators came out, and they did little more than add, subtract, multiply, and divide. By the time I graduated from college, Hewlett Packard had advanced calculator technology a lot. The testing center at the university I was attending was given some calculators to test in that environment. The calculators were programmable and made so people could beam information and programs to each other. The one problem that came out of this experiment was that students were cheating on exams, beaming test answers clear across the room. In response, HP reduced the range so calculators had to be right next to each other to make contact.

Later, when I became a teacher, these calculators became a mainstay in my math classroom. David, one of the most brilliant students I have ever had, had shown incredible skill in programming. I wasn't surprised when he took an interest in these calculators and came to me with some questions.

He showed me the one he had purchased. "Professor Howard, do you know how these transmit data?"

"Yes," I replied. "They transmit by infrared rays."

"Like a laser?"

"Kind of. But they are not amplified like a laser."

"But why do the calculators have to be so close to talk to each other?" he asked. "Doesn't a television remote use infrared? You can beam it clear across the room."

I told him the story about HP's experiment at the testing center when I was a student and how they had to reduce how far the calculators could transmit.

He smiled. "Good. That is just what I wanted to know. I was sure they had to be capable of it."

I made him promise that if he found a way to increase the signal that he wouldn't use it for cheating.

He laughed. "Oh, I won't do anything like that. I need it for something more important."

"What?" I asked.

"I'll let you know when and if I get it figured out."

David almost immediately took most of his calculator apart. I would come into the computer lab and find him working hard at it. He read and studied the manuals and other things he could get hold of. He analyzed each piece and considered what it did. Meanwhile, I kept reminding him to do his class work. One day I saw that his calculator was all put back together.

"Did you get it working?" I asked.

He nodded. "I think I've got it so it will beam about thirty yards. But I have to write a program to do some testing. I'll let you know once I have finished."

Again, I reminded him to do his class work.

A few days later he came to me and was absolutely excited. "It worked! The whole thing worked!"

"Good," I replied. "Now tell me what you did."

"Well," he said, "when I try to study in my apartment, my roommates have the television blaring so loud that I can't think. So after I increased the infrared range, I wrote a program that would record any infrared signal. Then I beamed the television remote and captured its signal into my calculator. Now, if they start watching television, I change the channel, turn down the volume—anything I want. My roommates have decided our television is possessed by an evil spirit, and now they go somewhere else to watch."

"You did all of this to change your calculator into a television remote?" I asked.

"Yeah, isn't it great?"

I smiled. "I suppose. But it might have been easier to have just gone to the library to study."

Calculator Music

David had shown his incredible skill in programming, but he was facing a problem staying in school. He was running out of money.

We talked about his options. Of course, I first suggested he apply for all of the scholarships he was eligible for. However, even if he were awarded one, it wouldn't take effect until the next semester, and he needed the money immediately.

"Have you considered using your programming skills?" I asked.

"In what way?" he asked in return.

"I've done database programs for financial institutions, network programs for companies, and written grade tracking programs for schools," I replied. "You might even be able to use your skills on the calculator to write programs teachers and students can use."

This last suggestion really intrigued him. "What kind of programs could a person write for the calculator?"

"I've written a few that can do financial or scientific calculations," I told him. "I even wrote one that plays music."

"Music? The calculator will play music?"

I nodded. "It will, but not very well—it has a very brassy sound. But just to see if I could do it, I wrote a program that plays the *1812 Overture*."

"Can I hear it?" he asked.

I pulled out my calculator, brought up the program, and hit play. As it played, he laughed.

"That's awesome," he said. "Can I have a copy?"

When the song finished, we set our calculators end to end and I beamed the program to him. He grinned as he played it. "This gives me an idea. Thanks for the help."

David spent the next few days visiting teachers in departments that used calculators the most. These included math, science, engineering, economics, and accounting. He got the teachers to share formulas with him that they would allow students to have programmed into their calculators. Once he had these, he set about writing the programs, and he put them into a package that the students could purchase.

A student could purchase the package for their individual class for only five dollars, or they could purchase the package that included everything for twenty dollars. He started making a fair amount of money, and students all over campus were talking about the wonderful calculator programs.

But students, as they are prone to do, started sharing copies with each other illegally, even though David had made them sign an agreement that they wouldn't. Watching students do this annoyed me because I knew David needed the money. But he didn't seem bothered at all. He just grinned when I asked him about it.

"When they copy it," he said, "it will work. But if I don't key a code in for them, certain keystrokes will make the calculator play music and display a cryptic warning reminding them to legally purchase the software."

"What keystrokes?" I asked.

"I found out which ones are used most often on tests, and those are what triggers the music," he replied.

A few days later, I was at the testing center working on a program for the testing center to transfer data from one computer system to another. While I was there, I heard and saw something that made me laugh. As different students took their tests, suddenly their calculators started playing the *1812 Overture*. Each time the music started, the student panicked and desperately tried to shut it off. The testing center would then make them relinquish their calculator and lend them a simpler model with which to finish their test.

It didn't take long for word to get around that a person really needed to pay for the code, and David soon had the money he needed for school.

As for me, every time I hear the *1812 Overture* start to play, I still tend to check my calculator.

Bum Lambs

The spring after I finished college, I was determined to spend more time with my little girls enjoying the farm life we had chosen. As I was outside one evening, I could see the lights of the lambing sheds in the distance, where the sheepherders worked around the clock helping the ewes birth their lambs. That gave me an idea.

"Annicka and Celese, would you like to have baby lambs?" I asked my three and four-year-old daughters. They never said yes directly, but their immediate squealing did. "I'm not promising anything until I talk to the men at the sheep camp," I told them. "I will go over there on Saturday."

I truly didn't plan to check about getting lambs until the weekend, but that night after I mentioned it, we could hardly get the girls to go to bed. They were far too excited. And it wasn't even six o'clock in the morning when they came bouncing into our room, waking us to ask if it was Saturday yet.

My wife, Donna, drowsily told me she thought it would be a good idea if I went over to the sheep sheds right away. Since we were already awake, I prepared to go to work. I decided to stop at the sheep sheds on my way, knowing they usually had someone on a shift around the clock. In this I wasn't disappointed. When I stepped inside the shed, two men were working there. I approached the first one and asked if they had any bum lambs.

Lambs can obviously be orphaned if the mother dies. However, a lamb can also be orphaned if a ewe has more than two, lambs. Her natural instinct is to push the extra ones away to ensure the survival of the two she chooses to keep. Usually the ones shoved away are the smallest. Lambs without a mother to take care of them are called bum lambs, and they can be fed on bottles. But most of the time the men are too busy to feed them, so the lambs don't make it.

The man I talked to said he was sure they would have some lambs I could have if I wanted to stop by after work. I made the mistake of calling Donna and telling her the news. She told the girls, and they drove her crazy the rest of the day.

I stopped at the farm store on my way home from work to get some milk replacer and some bottle nipples to fit on the end of pop bottles. I found a box in a dumpster and then drove to the lambing sheds. I was given two cute lambs that hadn't eaten for most of the day. I put them in the box in the front of my pickup and headed home.

When I got home, the minute Celese heard my door slam, she was there to look in the back of my pickup. Not seeing anything, her little eyes filled with tears.

"Daddy, I mad at you."

"Why don't you look in the front?" I said.

I opened the pickup door, and instantly the baaing of the hungry lambs could be heard. Immediately, Celese and Annicka were by my side. Soon they were each carrying a squirming lamb into the house to show their mother.

They wanted to play with the lambs, but I knew they needed food first. Donna mixed up some milk while I got the bottles ready. I funneled milk into each pop bottle and then put the nipples on. I tried to convince my daughters that I needed to feed the lambs until they got used to the bottles, but my daughters thought I was just being selfish. I finally gave up and handed them the bottles.

But a lamb, though small, is really strong. When the lambs couldn't figure out how to get milk from the bottle, they bunted my daughters, knocking them down. Then the lambs sucked on their clothes, trying to get the milk that had spilled on them. Finally, Celese handed me her lamb's bottle and turned to convince her younger sister to do the same.

"Annicka, let Daddy feed them," she said. "He's too big for them to eat him."

Lambs and a Dog

My little daughters loved their orphaned lambs that I had picked up at a sheep camp. After I trained the lambs to nurse on bottles, my daughters would march outside, bottles in hand, to feed their lamb babies. As the lambs ate, their little tails wagged happily back and forth.

After my girls took over feeding, I didn't do too much with the lambs. But one day when I came home from work, my five-year-old daughter came to me. I could see she had been crying.

"Yoda won't eat," she said through her sniffles.

When I came into the house, my wife, Donna, met me with a worried look on her face. "Neither lamb is well."

I immediately went to look at them and realized they had scours, a sickness that can be caused by many things, but it ultimately causes dehydration. There are pills to help overcome it, but the lambs can still be lost if they won't eat while the medicine is doing its job.

I immediately went and purchased some small pills for the lambs. Getting them to take the pills was another matter. After a few nipped fingers, I finally had them doctored, but they still wouldn't drink their milk.

A friend of mine worked at the sheep camp, so I went out there, hoping he would be on duty. He was, and as I stepped from my pickup, he waved.

"Hey, Howard, what brings you out here?"

"Just coming to see if you're staying out of trouble."

He laughed. "This time of year, I don't have time to get into trouble. If I get four hours of sleep each night, I count myself lucky."

"What I actually came for," I said, "is some advice. My two girls' little lambs have scours and aren't doing too well. We're struggling to get them to eat."

"I'm not sure I have any suggestions," he said.

"Is there anything the ewes do that encourages their lambs to nurse?"

He thought a minute and then smiled. "Well, they do lick their lambs' backsides, and that seems to stimulate their appetites." He laughed. "I suppose you could try that."

"Very funny," I said.

He didn't have any other suggestions, so I headed home. When I arrived, my little girls hurried out to meet me. Through their tears they told me that their mother didn't think the lambs were going to make it.

Donna was trying really hard to get the lambs to eat, but she wasn't having any luck. I told her what my friend had said about the ewe licking their lambs' backsides while they ate.

"You go ahead and try it, and we'll see how it goes," she said wryly.

She tried again to feed a lamb, and it not only refused to eat, but our new puppy pushed its way in to get petted. That made the bottle slip, and it sprayed milk across the back of the lamb. Immediately, our pup started to lick the milk off. When it did, the lamb perked up.

Donna looked up, and the glint in her eye told me she had an idea. She took the bottle and sprinkled milk around the lamb's tail. Our puppy started to lick it, and Donna offered the lamb the bottle. As long as the dog licked it, the lamb ate. Donna was able to get both lambs to eat this way. At the next feeding, Donna fixed three bottles, two for the lambs and one to sprinkle on them for the dog to lick.

The lambs started to flourish, and within a day or two they were bouncing around our yard. A few days later I ran into my friend who worked at the sheep camp. I told him about how Donna got the pup to lick the lambs and how that encouraged them to eat.

"That's great," he said with a grin. "But I really had hoped to hear how it went with you being the one to lick them."

What Winning Truly Is

I was twenty years old, living in New York far from home and spending long days working. So when the church congregation there decided to have a picnic, it was a great opportunity to relax and have a little fun.

There was lots of food. The ladies of the congregation had brought everything from fried chicken to apple pie. My colleague and I were offered places at the front of the food line, but just then, one of my favorite little people came to see me. Beth was four years old and acted like I was her hero.

When Beth's mother asked if she wanted some help getting a plate of food, Beth pointed at me and said, "I want him to help me."

Beth's mother looked at me questioningly.

I smiled and said, "I'd be happy to help her."

So instead of taking my place at the front of the line, I moved back by Beth. It took a bit of maneuvering, setting one plate down while I dished food onto the other, but eventually both plates were full. I carried them to a waiting table, and Beth climbed up on the bench by me, chatting happily as we ate. I loved to hear her little voice and have her share the important events of her life.

When dinner was over, there were lots of games. Though I wore a suit in my work, I took off my suit coat and tie and joined in. The final event of the day was a race. It was across the lawn, up a steep hill, along the ridge, and back down to the starting point. The prize was a big, beautiful, two-layered chocolate cake. Anyone of any age who wanted to could compete.

I endured lots of ribbing from the teenagers saying they hoped a fat, old man like me could actually finish the race.

I just said, "Very funny. Now prepare to be beaten!"

When the signal was given, I quickly jumped to the lead. By the time I reached the base of the hill, I was twenty yards ahead of the nearest competitor. I dashed to the top and looked back to find that the next runner wasn't even halfway up the hill. The hardest part for me was over. But then I saw something that made me stop. Beth, who was the smallest racer, had fallen only a short distance from the starting line.

I couldn't go on. Instead, I turned and headed back down the way I came, with the teenagers I passed laughing and joking that I was mixed up. When I reached Beth, I lifted her onto my shoulders and turned back to the race. By this time all of the teenagers had ascended the hill, and there was no hope of winning. So, with Beth holding tightly around my neck, I picked up the other two small children who were struggling their way toward the hill, tucked one under each arm, and raced much more slowly to the top.

By the time I reached the ridge, the first teenagers were crossing the finish line. I raced across the hill, and by the time I turned to descend, the last of the older children were finishing the race.

With the three children I was carrying urging me on with their laughter and cheers, I continued until, exhausted, I crossed the finish line in last place. The little children hugged me and laughed as everyone patted them on the back for running so fast. When I set the last child down and turned around, there stood almost everyone who was at the picnic. At the front were the teenagers, and leading them was the girl who had won. She held the cake out to me.

I shook my head. "I didn't win."

She smiled. "We all decided that in what really counts, you did win."

Then an old man spoke. "There is an old saying. 'It's not whether you win or lose that matters but how you run the race.' Today, you showed the right way to run."

I took the cake and said, "Then let's all share it."

As we all enjoyed it together, the cake tasted better than any cake could have if it had been won by crossing the finish line in first place.

A Superhero

I lived in New York when I was twenty years old, and the church I attended consisted mostly of divorced women with children. Unexpectedly, the woman who was responsible for the teaching of the children in the congregation, asked if I would consider working with them.

"I can see you love children," she said, "and these children could really use a good male role model."

I truly do love children, but the church assignment I had at the time made it difficult to work in that position. In addition, I needed special permission from church leaders. I told her I was willing if she could get permission. I really doubted she could get it, but I definitely underestimated her. Within the week I received a call from my ecclesiastical leader granting permission.

From then on, for as long as I lived there, I worked with the children. They ranged in age from three to twelve. My main assignment was to work with the boys who were eight and older, but I quickly learned what it meant to the other children to have me there. Whenever the whole group was together for an activity, the smallest children swarmed around me.

My favorite child was a little girl named Beth. Whenever I called her by name, her little face just lit up. She wanted me to help her with everything. She even insisted on having the chair right beside me during singing time even though I sat in the middle of all of the older boys.

I worked to learn each child's name and used it to greet them so they would know they were important to me. That seemed to mean the world to Beth. I hadn't realized how much so until one day when her mother called.

"Mr. Howard," Beth's mother said, "I want to ask a favor."

"What do you need?" I asked.

"Well, I really feel kind of silly asking this," she replied, "but I don't know of any way around it. You see, it's Beth's fourth birthday this week. We are having a birthday party for her, and we want to make it a special one. There is a place where a person can hire someone to come dressed as a Disney princess or a superhero. So we decided that was what we would do."

"That sounds like fun for her," I replied.

"The problem is," Beth's mother said, "is that we asked her whether she wants a Disney princess or a superhero, and she said she wants a superhero. We asked her which one she wants, and, well . . ."

She paused, seemingly embarrassed to say more, but finally she continued.

"She said she wants you." Beth's mother laughed nervously. "I tried to tell her that you aren't a superhero, and she got mad and said you are. I told her you are busy, but she said you told the children you always had time for them, and that's why you are a superhero."

My heart felt funny, thinking how this little girl viewed me.

Beth's mother continued, "Would you mind coming to a little girl's birthday party and being her superhero? I know it may seem weird since all of the other guests besides family will be a bunch of little girls, but if you could make time on Wednesday evening, it would mean the world to her."

"If I'm too busy to be there, then I'm too busy," I said. "I will make time."

I wanted to have a nice present for Beth, but I didn't know what a little girl would like. So before we hung up, I asked.

"You don't need to bring anything," Beth's mother replied. "Having you there is enough."

I insisted, so she gave me some ideas. I must admit that I felt awkward buying a pretty doll, but I found one I thought she'd like, and with my limited skills, I carefully wrapped it.

The night came, and I laughed as I wondered what my friends would think if they could see me sitting cross-legged on the floor drinking punch and eating cake with little girls at a tea party. But when the party ended and Beth gave me a big hug, I can honestly say that I actually knew what it meant to be a superhero.

A Cowboy and Some Special Horses

As I watched the veterans ride by on a big trailer in the Fourth of July parade, I was reminded of a good man I had grown to know and love.

I first met Bob the day the men from my church gathered to cut and haul wood for a widow in our community. I was twenty-five and the only one under fifty that showed up, so I was assigned the job of throwing the blocks of wood into the truck.

I would pick up one in each hand and fling them onto the load. After a while, I realized that Bob was intently watching me. He tried to grab a block of wood in one hand. Though his big, farm-roughened hands were the size of bear claws, due to age he didn't have the strength, and the wood slipped from his grasp.

He looked at me and smiled. "I used to be able to do like you do. But I don't see many young people anymore that can grasp a fifty-pound log and toss it into the truck like that."

"That's because they didn't grow up milking cows like we did," I replied.

"Did you work with horses, too?" he asked.

"Not as teams," I replied. "But I did ride a lot herding cattle."

"You ever heard of the Lipizzan horses?" he excitedly asked.

"Yes," I told him. "I read a book about the stallions and their rescue during World War II."

"The mares also needed rescuing," Bob said. "And I was able to be part of that. I was drafted into the war, and as a young private I found myself far from the farm, fighting in Patton's army. The death and destruction were unimaginable and took a mental toll on me.

"I fought in the Battle of the Bulge, losing many friends, and

I began to doubt whether we, as humans, had any redeeming qualities. Then our commander told us about allied prisoners of war and some special horses that were being held across the border in Czechoslovakia. We also received word of an advancing Soviet army, and our commander decided to attempt to free both the prisoners and the horses before the Soviets arrived.

"As we learned of our assignment, for the first time in a long time, I felt excitement for the mission we were attempting. For the most part, people welcomed us as we advanced, viewing our arrival as salvation of their beloved horses from destruction by the Soviet Army. The only problem we had came from stiff resistance by German SS troops near the border, but our tank division quickly crushed them.

"When we reached the town where the horses and prisoners were, instead of the fighting we expected from the German army stationed there, we were welcomed with an almost celebratory air. Not only were the American, British, and Polish prisoners of war happy to see us, but the Czechs, and even the German soldiers cheered us. All feared the advancing Soviet army and welcomed our protection of the horses that they were sure the Soviets would simply slaughter for food."

"The Germans welcomed you?" I asked in surprise. Bob nodded. "What was your assignment?" I asked.

"Because of my experience with horses, I helped load, transport, and even ride them to safety beyond the border. For the first time in a long time, I was able to renew my faith in the general goodness of people."

I enjoyed my visit with Bob, and as the years rolled by, I never forgot it. When Bob grew older and more feeble, I went to visit him. His good wife informed me that he didn't recognize anyone anymore. When I told him who I was, he looked blankly at me. As I visited, I reminded him of his story from years past.

Suddenly his eyes lit up.

"You're the guy that could throw a block of wood into the truck with one hand?"

When I nodded, he leaned back on his bed and spoke quietly.

"If you ever begin to doubt whether people have any redeeming value, just remember that in the midst of the ravages of war, men and women from opposite sides were able to set aside their differences and come together to save some beautiful horses." He then turned to me, smiled, and said, "Never forget that, and your faith in the goodness of mankind will never be destroyed."

And I have never forgotten.

A Beary Scary Tale

My university colleagues and I always tried to find summer work and then returned to share stories of our adventures. But John's story was unsurpassed that year.

As he had in other years, John found work in Yellowstone National Park doing trail maintenance. He walked the trails of the park with a chainsaw, cutting trees that had fallen across the paths. Also, as in previous years, because he would be working in the back woods, he had to sit through bear safety training even though he could nearly repeat it by heart.

Black bears seldom attack unless they think their cub is threatened. The best defense against them is to run away. It doesn't do much good to climb a tree because black bears can climb trees and do it much faster than a human.

Grizzlies are much more prone to attack. Grizzly cubs can climb trees, but grown grizzlies can't, so if a grizzly charges, if possible, find a sturdy tree to climb.

For all bears, make plenty of noise so you don't surprise them, and usually they will avoid human contact. If a bear does attack and you can't get away, roll into a ball to protect vital parts of your body and play dead.

John had just about tuned it all out when the head ranger said, "Be especially careful this year since we have had more grizzly sightings than in years past."

The summer work started out normally. There were a lot of trees downed by the heavy winter snows. John found the trees across the trail about every hundred yards. He didn't worry about making any additional noise, feeling the chainsaw made plenty. But after a few weeks on the job, he had one of the scariest experiences of his life. He came around a corner in the trail and there, about fifty yards from him, was a female grizzly.

He was surprised that she hadn't left the area when she heard the chainsaw. But when she turned and saw him, John knew he was in trouble and quickly sized up the surrounding trees. He didn't have long to consider options because she charged almost immediately. John ran to the best tree he could see. He reached it and was able to pull himself up into it just before she ripped out a chunk of wood below his feet. He climbed up until he knew he was safely out of her reach and sat down to wait until she left.

But that was where the bear training didn't work. The bear was supposed to prowl around the tree for a time and then leave. But this bear started shredding the base of the tree. John was grateful it was a strong tree, but he knew she would eventually topple it if she continued to rip it apart. He couldn't understand why she was so determined to get him. That is, he couldn't until he heard a cry from above him in the tree. John looked up, and to his horror he saw a grizzly cub ten feet up.

As the mother continued to rip the tree apart, he considered his options, and he suddenly knew what he had to do if he was to have any chance of survival. He climbed toward the cub, but the closer he came, the more the baby bear cried and the more viciously its mother attacked the tree. The baby bear moved as far out on a limb as possible to get away from him. Finally, as John felt the tree begin to shudder, weakened from the amount of wood ripped from its base, he moved within arm's length of the cub.

Holding tight to avoid falling, John reached his foot out and shoved the baby bear. It swiped at him, and when it did, he gave it a hard kick. It lost its hold and tumbled to the ground, landed on its fat backside, and bounced. The mother grizzly immediately ran to it. Then, to John's relief, the mother and cub ran away and disappeared into the woods.

John stayed in the tree for some time to make sure all was

safe and to slow his heart. Eventually, he climbed down, and, still shaking, he turned toward the path leading to the ranger station. When he reached it, he heard a loud crash. Thinking the mother bear had returned, he spun around. What he saw really made him tremble.

The tree he had climbed had fallen.

One Cat Is Enough

Jed wasn't fond of cats. So when his wife approached him about getting a kitten, he adamantly refused.

"Why do you think we need a cat around here?" he asked.

"Because I counted two mice in our house today," she replied. "And where there is one or two, you know there are more."

"We'll just set some traps," Jed replied. "Traps don't make messes or rip up the furniture."

But then Jed's little girls got into the act and begged and pleaded and looked at him with their big eyes, and soon Jed, in his opinion, owned one cat too many.

"But no more than one," he insisted.

The day Jed's wife brought home the little white ball of fur, Jed had to admit it was cute. "But I'm afraid it would lose in a fight with a mouse," Jed said. "The mice we have around here could eat it for lunch."

"It will grow," his wife replied.

It did grow, and it also grew fond of Jed. He wouldn't admit that he liked it, but more than once the others had caught him with it curled up on his lap. His older sons especially liked to tease him about it.

But then came the day that the now-grown cat came into heat. It seemed like every tomcat within a hundred miles was prowling around their house. Some were tame and underfoot, while others were vicious and acted like they owned the place.

"I think it's time for Snowball to be spayed," he told his family.

Though Jed was a cattle rancher, he was also a practicing veterinarian and planned to do the procedure himself. But that was where the trouble began. His little girls cried thinking of him hurting their sweet Snowball, and no amount of assurance that he would be careful helped.

"The only other option is to neuter all of the male cats," Jed said sarcastically.

Though Jed hadn't been serious, his little girls hugged him and thanked him for sparing their beloved cat.

Feeling trapped by his own words and unable to disappoint his daughters, he organized his sons into cat-catching patrols. They caught scores of tame cats, and while Jed worked to neuter those, the boys set out to trap the wild ones.

Jed suggested they put Snowball safely in a cat carrier at the back of the live-trap cage he had purchased to catch the raccoons that ravished their garden in the fall. They did, and the wild cats came by the dozens, even fighting to get into the cage. Though Jed was proficient and could take care of a cat in just a few minutes, the boys were still catching them faster than he could work his magic. They worked almost all day, and by the time the last cat wobbled its way out of the makeshift surgery, Jed was sure he had taken care of more than a hundred.

The cats all quickly fled the farm, deciding the price for romancing Snowball was a tad too high. Jed was sure there would be more cats the next day, but there weren't. There were none the next day or the next, and only one the day after that, which they quickly relieved of his romantic desires.

From then on, Jed marveled that no male cat ever came on their property again, even though he knew Snowball came into heat now and then. When he mentioned it to his oldest son, his son laughed.

"Well, Dad," he said, "if you were a cat and got word what happened when you came around our place, I bet you would reconsider whether or not you wanted to pay us a visit, too!"

The Write Pen

I always look forward to our family reunions, not only because I get to see all my family, but because I get to check out the newest technology. My brother David works in the tech industry, and one of his assignments is to test the newest computers to determine what items his employer should adopt.

As usual, he brought the latest computer, and as we sat outside under the trees, he let us try it. The screen came off, and it could function as a tablet or connect to a keyboard. The computer also had a full docking station. Its ram and hard drive space exceeded all of the computers I own combined.

Of course, for the price of it I could have made a couple of mortgage payments. The stylus alone was more than a hundred dollars, and it was nothing more than an expensive mouse in the shape of a pen.

Everyone was duly impressed—everyone, that is, except our mother.

When David asked her if she would like to try it, she said, "Just what would I use it for?"

David was silent for a moment, then his eyes lit up as he looked at Mom's journal. "With this computer," he said, "you can speak, and it will transform your speech into text. Just think how fast you could write your journal."

"But I don't want to talk my journal," Mom said. "I want to write it. What would I do with a talked journal?"

"But that's just the point," David said. "It transforms your speech into written text."

"And does it do it with my handwriting?" Mom asked.

"Well, no," David hesitantly replied.

"Then I don't want it," Mom said.

No amount of coaxing could encourage her to try it, so David finally set it down and joined in a rousing game of marshmallow war.

Meanwhile, Mom turned back to write in her journal.

"Shoot!" she said. "I forgot to get myself a pen."

"No problem," I replied. "I'll get one for you."

I had just gotten up when she informed me she had found one.

She tried to write in her journal for a while and then exclaimed, "This useless pen must be totally out of ink. I might as well take it inside and throw it away."

About that time, the game ended and everyone moved into the house to watch a movie. David walked over and picked up his computer, but as he looked all around, we could tell something was wrong.

"What's the matter?" I asked.

"I've lost my stylus," he replied.

We all looked for it, but it had disappeared. Suddenly my wife remembered Mom cussing the pen. Instantly, everyone knew where the stylus had gone.

David rushed into the house with the rest of us close behind. When he asked Mom about the stylus, she shook her head. "I haven't seen any—whatever you call it."

"Did you find a pen?" David asked.

"Only this worthless one that is out of ink," she said, pulling the stylus from her pocket. "I brought it in to throw it away."

"Ahhh!" David exclaimed. "That's my stylus. You can't throw it away."

Mom frowned and said, "That's sure a lot of fuss over a pen that doesn't even write."

Neighborly Neighbors

When Tina called, Sally could tell something was really wrong. Tina's voice was panicked and tense. She was so tense, in fact, that Sally couldn't understand what she was saying. Sally decided it would be best to walk to Tina's house and see what the problem was.

Tina was new to the area, and after she had moved in, she and Sally had quickly become friends. But they were about as different as two women could be. Tina had grown up in one of the roughest areas of a big city and had lived there all of her life. Sally had grown up on a big cattle ranch. Tina's high school graduation class was almost eight hundred students while Sally had thirty in hers.

Then Tina's husband, David, lost his job when the big inner-city school where he worked cut the music program. He found a new job in a little Idaho town and loved the friendliness of the small rural community. Tina seemed to enjoy it, too, but she was unsure about a lot of things.

Houses were quite a distance apart because everyone owned at least a couple of acres, so it was a fair walk to Tina's house. Sally hurried as quickly as she could. When she knocked on the door, Tina let her in and then looked nervously up and down the street as if she were worried that Sally might have been followed.

Once they were settled in Tina's living room, Sally asked, "So what's the problem?"

"I think I might have a stalker," Tina said nervously.

"What makes you think that?" Sally asked.

"Well," Tina said, taking a deep breath, "I went out to the car to drive to the store today, and when I opened the door, there was something in the car that someone must have left."

"Was the car locked?" Sally asked.

Tina shook her head. "I always lock it, but David has gotten so he doesn't. He used to where we used to live, but he feels so comfortable with everything here that he doesn't anymore."

"So what was left in your car?" Sally asked.

"A plate of chocolate chip cookies," came the reply.

Sally smiled. "Was there a note with them?"

Tina nodded. "There was. It said something like, 'Welcome to our town.'"

Sally laughed. "You don't have to worry about it, Tina. That's what people do around here. They share things with others. People will bake cookies and make some extra so they can take a plate to a neighbor. Quite often gifts are left anonymously. In fact, we have what we call 'The Neighborhood Plate.'. When you get something on it, your job is to refill it and pass it to someone without them knowing who left it."

"You mean the cookies that were left in my car aren't dangerous?" Tina asked in amazement.

"Only if you are on a diet," Sally said. "The ladies in our community are some of the best cooks in the world."

Tina went to her kitchen and came back with the cookies. They each ate one, and Tina laughed at her own nervousness.

"So do you always leave your car unlocked?" Tina asked.

"I usually do," Sally replied. "But not in the late summer and early fall."

"Why do you only lock it then?" Tina asked.

"Because that is harvest time," Sally replied. "And if you don't lock your car, you are likely to find it filled with zucchini someone wanted to share with you."

Tina laughed. "You know what? I think I'm going to like living here."

A Sinking Feeling About School

I walked into a local store and saw many aisles full of back-to-school supplies. The sheer volume caused me to remember a school in Peru.

We had gone to visit the floating islands of Lake Titicaca. The islands were fascinating. The first ones had been built when the Spaniards had taken over the country. Some of the Peruvians, not wanting to be ruled by the Spaniards, had moved out onto the lake. They built the islands and created their own little communities. But as the centuries passed and Peruvians gained self-rule, the Peru natives still continued to occupy the islands. I was fascinated to see how they lived. Though much of their livelihood now comes from tourism, at one time they subsisted on fishing and making small crafts they could sell on land.

The islands we visited never had more than four families, and most only had three. They didn't want too many, fearing that the weight would cause the reed-built islands to sink.

"Where do the children go to school?" I asked.

One of the natives, who spoke a fair amount of English, told me that there had been a school built on one of the islands. Each day the children from first through eighth grade would go there. It was the biggest island because families from all across the lake came together to build it. It only had one big reed building and a chalkboard. The children sat cross-legged on the floor as the teacher taught.

He also told me that it was always interesting sending the children off to school because, if there had been a big wind, the school would not be in the same place as the day before. Even though the islands were anchored, strong winds could still push them, anchor and all, across the lake. There were times they spent half of the day just finding the school.

If I understood his story correctly, after the school had been there for about ten years, the government did as many governments do. They decided that the school was not sufficient. It was decided that the children would each have a desk. Desks were provided, and the children, who were used to sitting on the floor, stacked them against the wall and continued sitting on the floor.

Then the government decided that the building was not sufficient, so the reed one was torn dow,n and a new one was built out of wood. Then the government felt that a single chalkboard wasn't enough, so more were added. Again and again something was deemed to be less than adequate, and something new was added.

Then one day, when the parents brought their children to school, it wasn't there. There had been no wind since the previous day, so they didn't know where it could have gone. After a brief search, someone noticed debris floating where the school had been. Upon closer inspection, everyone realized their school island had sunk.

The government took that as vindication of their concerns that the school and the island weren't good enough, but the locals knew it was the items the government forced upon them that caused the island's demise.

The children were excited to be out of school, and the man telling the story said his family decided to take the opportunity to visit relatives in Lima.

"But it didn't work out too well," he said. "Everyone wanted to know why our children weren't in school."

"Didn't you just tell them?" I asked.

"Yes," he replied. "But you see what strange looks you get when you tell people that your children can't go to school because it sank."

The Right Kind of Girl

Mike was telling me this week about meeting his wife, Melanie. He loved to go four-wheeling on the sand dunes near where we live, so his first date with any girl was to take her there to see if she enjoyed it as much as he did.

When he was set up on a blind date with Melanie, he, of course, took her there. After they had ridden in his dune buggy for some time, he asked her if she would like to drive. She nodded enthusiastically, so he turned it over to her.

"Let me explain everything," he said, pointing to the different parts of the machine. "This lever is the clutch. This one is the brake. This one is . . . "

"Mike," she said, interrupting him, "I've got this."

"Okay," he replied. "Let's see what you can do." Then, as she gunned the machine forward, he yelled over the roar, "You will want to stay on the small hills until you feel comfortable with everything."

Mike was quite sure that she rolled her eyes at his suggestion, and the next thing he knew they were sailing up one of the biggest hills. She drove, holding the machine to the steep sides of the dune better than any girl he had ever seen. In fact, if he were honest, he might even have to admit she was better than he was. But one thing he did know for sure; as far as he was concerned, he had found the right kind of girl for him.

As he told his story, I thought about how I would take girls I dated to the ranch where I grew up. Farm and ranch life can be dirty, sweaty, and tiring, but there is nothing like hard work and life outdoors.

I had taken city girls to the ranch before and shared what my life was like. Most of the time they were happy when we left and wouldn't go out with me again. Still, if I developed a relationship with a girl, I felt she needed to understand what kind of man I was.

When I met Donna, I was immediately drawn to her. She and I may have been different in about every way imaginable, but she was not afraid to try something new. We had dated for a while, so I decided it was time to take her to the ranch. I did so with great trepidation, considering how it had turned out with the other girls.

When we arrived at the ranch, I gave Donna a pair of coveralls to put on to keep her clothes clean. Then we went out to milk the young cow that provided milk for our family.

The cow was very gentle, so I would just take a bucket of grain out to the pasture and call her. She would come, and I would tie her to the nearest tree and milk her.

I showed Donna how to milk, and she struggled for a bit but was soon getting a good stream. As we both milked, I squirted her. The milk dripped down her coveralls, and she laughed. She decided to see if she could get me back, but I figured I was safe since she was new at it. I was wrong. She sprayed milk at me, hitting me in the chest. I was surprised, and she was proud of herself. She laughed and moved out about twenty feet, thinking there was no way I could hit her at that distance.

But I have milked cows most of my life, and I sprayed a stream of milk that hit her right in the face. That was the big test, and Donna laughed. With all of the commotion, the cow kicked over the bucket, causing Donna to laugh even harder. She didn't rush to get away, but helped me calm the cow and finish milking.

That was when I knew I had found the right kind of girl for me.

If you enjoyed our book, we would love to have you do a review on Amazon at:
http://amzn.com/1629860069

Would you like to see *Life's Outtakes* column running in your local paper or magazine? Suggest it to the editor. If an editor runs the *Life's Outtakes* column due to your suggestion, we will send you one of Daris Howard's books of your choice, signed by the author. Find out more at:
http://www.darishoward.com

Read other stories, purchase more books, or sign up for a short story each week by going to
http://www.publishinginspiration.com

Other books
by
Daris Howard
Daris Howard Amazon page:
http://amzn.com/e/B004H76UGK

For inspiring plays and books, as well as discounts for book sellers, go to
http://www.publishinginspiration.com

About the Author

Daris Howard is an author and playwright who grew up on a farm in rural Idaho. He associated with many colorful characters, including cowboys, farmers, lumberjacks, and others. Besides his work on the farm, he has worked as a cowboy and a mechanic. He was a state champion athlete and competed in college athletics. He also lived for eighteen months in New York.

Daris and his wife, Donna, have ten children and were foster parents for several years. He has also worked in scouting and cub scouts, at one time having eighteen boys in his scout troop.

His plays, musicals, and books build on his many experiences and the characters of those he has associated with to bring his work to life.

Daris is a math professor, and his classes are well-known for the stories he tells to liven up discussion and to help bring across the points he is trying to teach. His scripts and books are much like his stories, full of humor and inspiration.

He and his family have enjoyed running a summer community theatre, where he gets a chance to premiere his theatrical works and rework them. His published plays and books can be seen at http://www.darishoward.com. He has plays translated into German and French, and his work has been done in many countries around the world.

In the last few years, Daris has started writing books and short stories. He writes a popular news column called *Life's Outtakes* that consists of weekly short stories and is published in various newspapers and magazines in the United States and Canada, including *Country*, *Horizons*, and *Family Living*.

www.ingramcontent.com/pod-product-compliance
Lightning Source LLC
Chambersburg PA
CBHW060630130626
46555CB00002B/735